THE PEOPLE'S CITY

In support of the OneCity Trust

Foreword by
Frank Ross, The Rt. Hon. Lord Provost
of the City of Edinburgh

Introduction by
Irvine Welsh

First published in
Great Britain in 2022 by Polygon,
an imprint of Birlinn Ltd.

Birlinn Ltd
West Newington House
10 Newington Road
Edinburgh
EH9 1QS

www.polygonbooks.co.uk

9 8 7 6 5 4 3 2 1

ISBN 978 1 84697 601 8
EBOOK ISBN 978 1 78885 485 6

British Library Cataloguing-in-Publication Data
A catalogue record for this book is available on
request from the British Library.

Typeset in Bembo by Polygon, Edinburgh
Printed and bound in Great Britain by Clays Ltd, Elcograf S.p.A.

CONTENTS

FOREWORD

It gives me great pleasure to see the fourth anthology to be published in aid of the OneCity Trust; along with the continued support of three of Edinburgh's most famous authors and original contributors from our first book, *OneCity,* published in 2005.

In 2022, I welcome the addition of three female authors, who all, through their own personal connection to Edinburgh, add their unique writing style to this eclectic collection of stories. The reader will be enraptured by this anthology of short stories, and its Edinburgh landmarks, the majority of which are set in times gone by and add a historical twist that make the book hard to put down.

The aim of the first book in 2005 was to promote the message through the OneCity Trust that Edinburgh 'should no longer be a divided city but one city with one voice'. Sixteen years later, and the division remains evident from a report published in 2020 by the Edinburgh Poverty Commission, 'A Just Capital: Actions to End Poverty', which finds that over 77,000 citizens are living in poverty, including one in five children. This shows an increase of over 25 per cent in the last five years.

The impact of the COVID-19 pandemic has also caused great hardship to many in the city, bringing increased unemployment, the need for food banks, along with a decline in mental health. Data poverty has increased also as the world turns to online meetings as a way to communicate with others. Schools used online teaching methods with children; yet some homes didn't have access to the internet or adequate equipment. The inequalities have been huge, and the pandemic has exacerbated the divide in society.

The OneCity Trust has been fortunate to work with a number of key organisations over the past six years to deliver community benefit funding to projects in the city. The support of the City of Edinburgh Council, Travis Perkins Managed Services, CGI UK Ltd, ENGIE, CCG (Scotland) Ltd and City Fibre has seen tens of thousands of pounds being distributed to local communities. Together, we will work to end the inequality and poverty which continues to divide our city, with a vision that, one day soon, we will have a Thriving, Welcoming, Fair and Pioneering city for one and all.

I would like to thank all of the authors for giving their time and story writing talents to our book; the OneCity Trust is indebted to you. To Travis Perkins Managed Services and Morrisons Energy Services, thank you for your financial support which has helped us produce this book. To our readers, thank you for purchasing this book, which will raise funds for the OneCity Trust to continue its legacy to make Edinburgh 'OneCity'.

Frank Ross, The Rt. Hon. Lord Provost
of the City of Edinburgh

INTRODUCTION

Since I contributed to the first OneCity Trust book in 2005, I'm sorry to say not much has changed in our city – or in society as a whole.

The poorest parts of Edinburgh are still characterised by underemployment, low wages, and insufficient access to essential services, as deprivation thrives exponentially, passed down from generation to generation like a devastating disease. Now more people than ever before have been pulled down onto the breadline, with many more households struggling to make ends meet as benefits are continually cut and community funding is slashed. Working people that might once, fifteen or twenty years ago, have been considered middle class, are now shackled with debt, as proven by the lengthy queues outside food banks.

These issues stem from the fact that in places like our capital – a global tourist attraction – the focus has shifted from serving the needs of locals to feeding the bottomless trough of neoliberal capitalism. Therefore people are largely deigned not to exist in a city increasingly redesigned to attract tourists, wealthy students, businesses, and housing developers. The people who bring income are paramount, and our modern culture of cheap Airbnb accommodation, landlordism and commercial development constantly feeds the dominant narrative telling us that so-called 'legacy citizens' are irrelevant to the city's progress. They are simply displaced casualties of an economic, social and technocratic order that says they have no relevance in the modern world. After all, if Edinburgh does not court the international market, politicians argue, another city will simply take its place, with the income and investment going to other communities around the world.

In short, the people who actually live in Edinburgh, especially in our poorer communities, are at best forgotten, at worst ignored.

Government agencies and the poverty industry are not friends of our communities. All major transnational bodies, governments local and national, and all major political parties, are accepting of an economic system that sees poverty as a (regrettable or otherwise) consequence of the enrichment of the already super-wealthy. Whether their posturing is 'national' or 'global' such agencies are basically the hirelings of the one per cent. Therefore, any attempts to challenge this paradigm are piecemeal and token, with progressive policies rarely scratching the surface of such systemic issues.

So, what can be done to ensure this damaging legacy doesn't continue decade after decade? I believe it is time we accept that the state is no longer the driving force for change. It has become purely a tool of capital, and now cannot have a role in redistributing power and wealth through the society and community it purports to represent. Therefore our citizens have to find the voice and the confidence to start putting their own structures in place – and there has never been a better time to do it. The fact that football fans now feed their local communities through at-turnstile-collections for food banks, and that organisations like Helping Hands brought sport and recreation back into the schemes, tearing some children from screens and a future of morbid obesity, shows that the problems of the community have their solution in the community. A disinterested state, run only to service the needs of the untaxed global and national wealth-looters, will only, at best, offer crumbs on a grudging whim. Our citizens need to take the power and responsibility for their own destinies into their own hands.

Over the past 18 months or more, the pandemic has highlighted the existing inequalities that already plagued our neighbourhoods, shining a spotlight on the hunger, debt and hardship that goes unacknowledged in the mainstream media and political parties (unless through some token pious bleating as they assume the neoliberal agenda). In the middle of a time when family and friends were pushed achingly apart, communities rallied together, installing vital safety nets that the Government had, year after year, pulled out from under them. People were given a glimpse of what our society could look like if we lived in a more benign world that actually put people first, and that is a legacy we need to build on and help flourish.

As a writer, I naturally believe art and culture is vital for encouraging this empowerment to take root. In low employment and low economic areas, the arts are the only real way people can express themselves, and that's why projects like the OneCity Trust book are so important. The purpose of this collection of stories, just like the last, is to encourage people to have the confidence to express themselves. Because doing this involves articulating your own needs and taking action to meet them.

So while angry that the great welfare state, constructed after the horrors of the Second World War, has been decimated and warped beyond repair by the super-wealthy, I'm proud to be associated with a venture that is about art and culture – another one of the casualties of a neoliberal order that reduces them to profitable entertainment.

Brian Eno once said: 'culture is what you do when you do what you want to do, rather than what you have to do.' We citizens are now irrelevant to the super-rich and their state. The system needs to dupe us into giving it our seal of legitimacy every five years or so. That's about the extent of our participation in the decisions that affect our lives. But the good news is that they are irrelevant to us. They either can't or can barely offer us work or food. We can now do that for each other, and spend more time doing what we want to do. First we have to learn how to be free. Art and culture is how we do this.

Irvine Welsh

The Finally Tree

ANNE HAMILTON

MONDAY

I've found him, Ali. But . . .
    But.

There was always going to be a but, and it was always going to be a big one. Alina wondered which of the big three D's it would be. Dead. Demented. Dispossessed. An irreverent trinity that she'd found fitted most of life's 'buts'.

On Inverleith Row, she checked the time and saw she was early; she always was. This was a pilgrimage. The plane, a train to Waverley, then the bus skimming the New Town, all were fuelled on her anticipation of entering the East Gate through its magical scent of nostalgia and anticipation.

I've found him, Ali. But . . . It was the soundtrack to her long journey home. Even as she'd dozed, read, stared from screen to window and back again, the rhythm propelled her: de dah de dah de dah; *I've found him, Ali but*; de dah de dah de dah. Unconsciously, she'd tapped her toes in time with it.

She bent to pick at a scraggly dandelion pushing through the cracks in the pavement. She blew on the fragmented petals, then gently separated them and began counting: *Fin's found Jamie, he's found him not, he's found him, he's found him not . . .*

It had to be that, didn't it? And, of course there was a *but*. Anyone who disappeared for twenty-five years returned with A Story. If they returned at all.

Alina had never in twenty-five years regretted her decision that Fin should be adopted, never. Other events from back then she did question, though, and that text, that *but*, quite possibly meant she had been found out. Fin had been looking for his birth father for nigh on ten years, now, and naïve or stupid, as time rolled on without news, she'd learned to live with the risk.

'Ali . . .Ali . . .? *Alina.*'

The voice penetrated. When she looked up, there he was, Fin, coming towards her. He reminded her of Jamie she realised with shock: floppy blond hair, and slim. Even down to the leather jacket – or was her mind playing tricks? Wishful thinking, perhaps. She put up her hand to wave and stood waiting.

'Ali. I thought I was going to have to chase you round and round the gardens and in and out the dusty bluebells.'

'Sorry, I was miles away. How are you? Is everything okay?' Alina searched his face; he looked nothing other than pleased to see her.

'Everything's fine.'

'Really?' *I've found him Ali, but* . . . Surely this was the – first – moment of truth. 'Really, Fin?'

'Oh, you mean my text?' Yes. So, er, did my "but" look big in that, Ali?' He raised one eyebrow, his party trick; Alina couldn't do it.

'Oh, very funny.' She relaxed slightly and leaned in to hug him.

'Coffee?' he asked. 'Inside or takeaway?'

A smattering of rain picked up speed, helped by a sudden gust of wind, and Alina shivered. A quick glance up at the sky, leached of all colour, made up their minds and they crossed towards the café.

'You grab that.' Fin suggested, gesturing to a table at the edge of the busy room. 'I'll queue. Latte, right?'

'Please.'

There was always a moment at the Botanics, jet lagged or not, afraid her life was about to implode or not, when the years fell away and Alina was in limbo between past and present. It was here, seventeen years ago, that she'd met Fin for the first time. She'd been horribly nervous then, as well, worried that this unknown little boy would be bored, mooching ahead with his hands in his pockets and scuffing his feet. After all, it was one thing to know you had a birth mother on the fringes – Fin's was an open adoption: cards and gifts twice a year; annual school photograph; holiday postcard – another to give up a precious afternoon to the stranger she was. But Alina had underestimated Fin, and the powerful mix of logic and curiosity that made up his eight-year-old self.

'We come here a lot, maybe every week,' he'd told her, dumping his dinosaur backpack on the ground and rooting in it. 'Do you?'

'I used to, when I lived in Edinburgh.' She'd hesitated, then, wondering whether to add that this was where she'd first met his birth father, but it seemed too much too soon.

'Me and my dad made a map so I can show you my favourite things. Look.' Fin held up a jagged scroll tied with a piece of ribbon.

'Like a treasure hunt?' she'd asked. 'I love treasure hunts.'

'Me too.'

Unfurling the map and following its crayoned dotted lines, had broken the ice, and they paced the paths, crossing ornamental bridges, like the ghosts of Victorian gentlefolk, politely discussing how to seek out the tiny rhododendrons hiding in the Rock Gardens.

'I don't know what a rhododendron looks like,' Alina had whispered, truthfully, and he'd patted her arm with the gravity of a little old man. 'It's okay, we're all learning together – that's what my teacher says.' Fin had marched her to the glasshouses next, giddy in the arid lands and the tropical rainforest, daring her to believe in red pineapples and the promise of early morning tree frogs. He'd flagged a bit then; he was hungry. 'Have you got a sneaky snack in your bag? I'm not asking for sweeties.' He'd squinted hopefully. 'But sometimes when people meet for the first time they do bring sweeties, don't they?'

When she'd produced a big bag of stupidly expensive be-ribboned jelly beans she'd picked up just in case, his eyes lit up with such glee, she glimpsed the toddler she'd never known, all red wellies and Paddington duffle coat. He ripped the bag open and shared the ones he hadn't spilled, counting out – sternly equally – the sugary jewels into their hands.

Alina smiled now, re-tracing that first journey with the comfort that Fin's memories were as rosy-glowing as her own. Two, then three, four, and increasingly more times a year they met here, regular as the seasons, solid as the earth from which the magnificent gardens grew.

'Here you go.' The grown-up Fin snapped back into focus as he set a mug of coffee and a slice of millionaire's shortbread in front of her. 'Thinking back?' he said with a grin.

Alina nodded. 'Daydreaming, really. Jet lag, too.'

Fin sipped his drink. 'I bet. How is work?'

'All good. Hoping we're robust enough to avoid this coronavirus thing, but . . .' She shrugged.

'Yeah. Aren't we all.' Fin pulled a face. 'Kind of puts things into perspective.'

Did it though? *I've found him, Ali, but* . . . She settled on a non-committal, 'Hmm.' In the ensuing silence, she looked down at the table, rearranging her cup, then his, two spoons and a plate, until they were in perfect alignment. She knew Fin's eyes were on her. 'So,' she said, meeting them.

'So.'

They looked at one another for a long, long second.

'You've found him, then,' Alina said. 'Jamie.'

'Ye-es.' Fin looked . . . not angry, not disappointed, but perplexed.

Hopefully, it *was* just one of the big three D's. Ah, no, Alina retracted the thought half-heartedly, she didn't mean that, but she had to know what she was working with. She'd start at Ground Zero: 'He's dead, isn't he?'

Fin folded his arms and sighed. 'No. Well, yes. In a way.'

Ah, thought Alina. The Story.

'The thing is . . .'

She watched him search for the words. Was he protecting himself, or her? Both of them, perhaps.

'Ali, Jamie doesn't exist anymore.' It wasn't like Fin to be oblique.

'I don't understand,' she said.

'I've found my birth father who isn't my birth father.'

'*What*?' Alina knew immediately she'd over reacted. 'Sorry. Go on.'

'Look. In a sense, he is alive and well, but—' Fin grinned faintly; Alina was too wound up – '*but*, there's no easy way to tell you this.'

For the first time in forever, she wanted to snap at him. She bit it back, well aware it was Jamie she was irritated with. No, it wasn't; it was herself. 'Go on?'

'Ali, for the last eight years, Jamie's been known as Sanna.'

'Sanna?' Alina's brow creased.

'Yes. Jamie, my birth father, is now Sanna. He's been living as, I mean he *is*, *she* is, a woman.'

Alina picked up her empty cup and pretended to take a drink. Then another. The shock on her face was genuine, easily masking the little trickle of relief. 'Right,' she said, nodding slowly, mind whirling. 'Right. What else?'

'Er, most people might think that was enough, Ali.' After a few seconds, Fin went on. 'She's an academic, apparently. A professor.'

'Jamie? He's a *professor* – of what? You're joking?' Alina hastily wiped the smirk from her lips; to laugh felt inappropriate. More relief slipped through.

'No, Ali.' Fin's voice was gentle. 'Sanna is.'

'God. Yes, of course. Right. Sanna.' Crockery rattled around them. The hiss of the coffee machine sounded like an exploding boiler. The world tilted for a second.

Whatever Alina had expected, it wasn't that. Being transgender didn't fit into the three Ds. It was something to be celebrated, surely. It was . . . Alina stopped, stumped. She didn't know what it was. And not only that, but a professor, of all things. 'Is that it? Any more surprises?' She held her breath.

'That's it.'

'I don't know what to say,' she admitted.

'I know you don't. Neither did I.' Fin shook his head. 'You don't have to be poker-faced and unshockable. I wasn't. It is bloody weird.'

Alina gathered her wits, trying to recalibrate. She hadn't been found out. Yet. 'How do you feel?'

'I'm fine now, I think.' Fin picked up the cup in front of him and swirled the cooling dregs around as if he were reading tea leaves. He paused and looked up as if assessing his feelings. 'Yeah, I am. I mean, that somebody got in touch in the first place is really the biggest shock, you know.' He sat back. 'It's not as if I've been looking for my dad, is it? I've got a great dad.' He spoke more fluently now, and Alina knew this was rehearsed, he'd been over it and over it, making sense of it – that was Fin; that was *her* too.

'Are you going to meet her?'

'I want to, but . . .'

Alina's heart flipped a beat. Was this where it all fell down? 'All right,' she said. 'What?'

'She, Sanna, wants to see you first.'

'Me? Why?'

'I don't know. Apparently, she said it would probably make sense to you. Does it?' Fin looked at her hopefully. 'Will you meet her?'

'Oh . . . Yes. Yes, of course, I will.'

'Great. I knew you would, Ali.'

His trust in her made her want to cry; she didn't deserve it. Neither did he notice she hadn't answered his first question, and they sat in silence for a few minutes. Alina felt weak. It was the jet lag, just the jet lag.

Fin stood up and held out his hand. 'Come on, you look shattered. You should be at home.'

'But the gardens, the Finally Tree, Fin. We always . . . I mean, don't you want—'

'Ali. The tree has been here tens if not hundreds of years. It'll be here after we're gone. It's not the Faraway Tree, waiting to change worlds.'

It was a bit, though. Alina slowly stood up, placing her bag over her shoulder. 'I need to sleep,' she agreed, embracing the firmer ground. 'It seems like days since I got here.'

'Are *you* okay, Ali? I mean, Jamie was,' Fin hesitated, '*is* your past.'

'My past. Exactly.' If only he knew. Alina mustered a proper smile. 'I'll be fine, Fin. I just need to take it in. Your "but" may have looked big in the text but it certainly didn't look anything like this.'

'Things change, Ali. People change.'

But they didn't, not in the time warp in Alina's mind. 'I'll always be your baby's father, Alina,' he'd promised, when they'd made their pact all those years ago, 'I'll never change.' But that had been Jamie.

Where was it going to leave the three people they had become?

1994

Pure luck had seen Alina accepted into Edinburgh University at the same time as Jamie. They were from different worlds.

'People like me don't go to university,' Alina had said cheerfully.

'People like me always do but it doesn't mean we should,' Jamie countered.

Both were out of step rather than out of their depth. It wasn't a case of looking back and realising it, they'd always known it. Jamie seemed to live far more in the moment than everyone else around them, Alina included. Even at nineteen – at nine, if she were honest – she'd been a planner, which served her well, but Jamie made her appreciate the here and now and, if there was no appreciation to be had, they poked fun at it, and the moment got better. It was his irreverence she cherished, in this strange student world where political correctness and straight-talking overlapped like a weird Venn diagram, foreign to the housing scheme she'd grown up in.

The first time she had seen Jamie was at a cross-discipline lecture for Social Work (her) and Computer Science (him) students, eyeing each other up like alien species. The second time, they'd noticed each other at the Botanics, wryly bonding in such a non-student-like environment. Geographically, both lived near-ish: Alina with her grandparents in Granton ('the wrong end,' she parroted to Jamie, whose head it went over) and Jamie in Trinity, where his parents had bought him a flat ('I asked them not to,' he stressed).

'Can I be your partner in those cross-dressing classes?' he asked, making her giggle. 'I'm an out-and-proud nerd, and very scared of your lot.'

'Yes, please. I'm scared of them too.' She'd taken out a marker and drawn a smiley face on each of their hands to cement the deal.

'Are they always that uptight?' he'd asked.

'Hmm. Nobody cried today.' It had started to drizzle and Alina was busy shoving her notebook into her bag. 'That's a first.'

'Ha ha . . . Wait, you're serious? For fuck's sake.' He'd tried to purse his lips into a whistle but was trying too hard not to laugh.

'Sadly not.' Alina found his grin infectious. 'What makes you think I'm not the chief crier?'

'Algorithms. I'm a computational physics genius and I worked out the probability.' They walked out the gate, and turned left together. 'Joke. It was your shoes.' He pointed down at her feet, then his own. 'Same as mine. It was a sign.'

Alina followed his gaze; well, they both wore trainers that fitted somewhere on a large spectrum of 'red'. He'd found a nice way of not saying they were both plain ordinary.

Jamie was an only child, too, fresh from boarding school, and Alina suspected they had found a sibling in each other. There was certainly no physical spark between them. They were, they agreed, useless at being students, united in a silliness that was an outlet for both of them; together they didn't have to fight the world. With Jamie, choosing a KitKat in the cafeteria didn't have to become a full-on tirade against Nestlé, or a passing remark about a wedding invitation, an earnest discussion about religious institutional oppression.

MONDAY

In retrospect, Alina was relieved she'd grown up more socially and politically aware, more tolerant – as presumably, had Jamie given that he . . . no, not he, Sanna, was free to be Sanna – but she could forgive their nineteen-year-old selves a means of coping.

Jamie had known all about Fin before he disappeared. Well, not Fin exactly, but about the baby boy whose name they had picked together. That's when he'd made his promise.

'I'll always be your baby's father, Ally-Bally.' *Ally-Bally.* 'Always.'

Alina recalled having had one of those old telephone trolleys wheeled over to her in the maternity ward, so she could phone him. The midwife had offered to do it, not believing it wouldn't render Alina jelly-like and tearful. In fact, she felt invincible. She'd done it: a textbook pregnancy, giving birth to a perfect healthy baby. It had been hard, very hard, but not impossible. Nothing ever would be after that.

And it hadn't been, until now. Meeting Fin for the first time had come close, but not very. From where she stood at present, though, something about that made Alina wince. Had she been smug? Self-righteous, even? Playing God with half a dozen lives before benevolently handing over her gift of a baby.

Well, this was payback time.

She'd waved Fin off on the street, psyching herself up to climb the four flights of stairs to the flat. Once there, Alina went to bed and slept for fifteen hours straight. In the morning, nothing was clearer, but she felt the tuggings of the grim resilience that had always carried her through. The worst had happened; she just had to take back control.

'Is it wrong to admit I've Googled her, Ali? Looked on Twitter and Facebook,' Fin had asked.

Alina thought it the obvious thing to do, and said so. Hadn't she done the same, in idle moments, usually around the time she ran a speculative eye over notes in the Edinburgh University alumni magazine, or in more recent years, its LinkedIn profile. She'd been looking for a deadname, though, not a female professor, for God's sake. Fin had had no luck either. 'I'm guessing he . . . she might have changed her surname when she, er, transitioned,' he'd suggested. It seemed a fair point.

'Come on, then, let the real contestant show themselves,' Alina muttered to herself as she threw back the covers and got out of bed. Since it seemed that a Corona-related lockdown was inevitable, she and Fin had agreed to meet up again quickly, the following day, and his first question would be, had Jam— had Sanna been in touch. *Oh, shit.* Alina's stomach sank, *please* don't let them have to do a three-way reunion via Skype or that Zoom thing.

It gave her the impetus to attack her Gmail inbox. Working for a fledgling NGO, spending half the year overseas, meant junk accumulated, occasionally masking a gem, so Alina scrolled carefully and deleted ruthlessly. She was left with a couple of personal messages, and a handful from legitimate-looking but unknown, accounts: *delete, delete* – Alina paused suddenly, mid-click, and went back. She stared at the sender's address: s.andrews1@midyork. ac.ed.uk.

That had to be it. The subject header simply said 'Meeting'. She frowned, conscious of her heartbeat pounding. 'Well, open it, you idiot,' she muttered to herself. She didn't though; methodically, she carried on until she'd emptied the inbox and composed some replies, her hands shaking as they hovered over the keyboard. Then she double-clicked.

The email *was* from Sanna, of course it was. Alina ran her eye over it quickly, needing to know the bad news. Then, reassured there absolutely was nothing 'bad', she went back to the beginning and started again; a third time:

Dear Alina,
A promise is a promise, isn't it, even after twenty-five years. Can we meet up? You'll know from Fin that I'm Sanna now, and I think you might just

take that in your stride. What you'll find it harder to accept is that I'm a – wait for it – university professor of – wait for it again – Peace Studies. Yes, you read that right. You can laugh, but better if we laugh together?

So. The-place-where-it-all-began? If we seize the day, I can come to Edinburgh, before the world gets quarantined. *We need to talk*, as they say.

Love, Sanna (Andrews) neé Jamie (Drew) x

It was like hearing Jamie's voice. Shockingly so. Alina put her hand to her mouth to suppress an involuntary sob, but just as quickly she was laughing through her tears. He'd – *she'd* – got it so, so right. Alina did a quick calculation, and recklessly ('Me, reckless. Imagine,' she murmured out loud) chanced her arm:

Hi Sanna,
Friday? The weekend? You choose. Of course, the-place-where-it-all-began. Where else? If it's not too far for you to travel. We can talk. And there's something you should see.
Love Alina x
PS Wear red shoes.

She'd done it. Alina sat back heavily and sighed. She'd done it. But *what* exactly had she done? She dithered, wondering whether to look up the college website and find Sanna's profile – of course she was curious to see how she'd changed; Sanna was probably sitting at her desk wondering the same thing about Alina – but she didn't do it, not yet. She just wasn't ready. What to tell Fin, she wondered. *When* to tell him, before or after the event? She hadn't an answer to that yet, either.

Instead, she went back to bed and slept some more, dreaming she was shoe-shopping, with not a red pair to be had.

WEDNESDAY

'I've got cold feet.' Fin hunched inside his coat like a teenager.

Briefly, Alina wasn't sure if he meant it literally. The afternoon had grown chilly, more autumn than spring, and with a threatening spit of rain in the air. Unusually there was no wind, though, and the Botanics felt still, as if waiting.

'Which one?' She said it lightly, no big deal. It worked; the agitated look in his eyes made space for the quizzical.

'The weather, the Finally Tree, your birth father, or none of the above?' Alina elaborated.

'Can I have all of them?'

'Free with a jelly bean.' Alina produced a crumpled packet, and ripped the corner off. 'They're Co-op. Not the fancy ones I bought when you were eight, but we can't visit the Finally Tree without jelly beans, it would be like Christmas without a tin of Quality Street. Here.' She shook them into his cupped hands.

'Thanks, Ali. I knew you'd talk me down,' Fin said.

It didn't happen often because very little fazed the calm

and grounded Fin, he'd always been that way, but Alina wanted to gather him into the type of hug suited to a six-year-old who had just been tripped up by the big bad world.

'Let's just disappear into the past for a bit, shall we?' Alina suggested. 'Fingers crossed we can find it,' she added, as she always did.

'Ah, Ali, have faith. We always find it,' he said as *he* always did.

'Shall we walk the longest way round?' Alina suggested. 'It's too cold for anyone not wearing thermals to want to sit down under a tree today. And, you don't want literal cold feet to add to the metaphorical ones.'

'I'm not sure why I've got such a . . . wobble on.' Fin pulled the collar of his jacket up. 'I mean, nothing's changed.'

'You had to tell me. You didn't know how I'd react. Maybe that hit a nerve. The mind's a funny thing.' Alina shrugged. 'If we rein ourselves in too tightly we're bound to blow up sometime. Or something like that. I'm not a psychologist.'

'You're a social worker, though. Or you were.'

'Makes shite all difference.' Alina looked around at the trees and shrubs. There was little colour, everything still looked blanched and sodden from the ravages of a winter not yet yielding to spring. It had to come soon though, Easter was around the corner.

'Like, is she my birth father?' Fin stopped.

Alina's step faltered, and when she spoke it was carefully. 'What do you mean?'

'Just that. How can I meet her when I can't get the

language right?' Fin carried on, not noticing Alina's responses. 'Is she my birth mother, now, as well as you? Do I have two?' He looked towards the sky and took a deep breath. 'See? What do I call her?'

'Co-parent? Better still, ask her what she wants.' Here, Alina was confident. 'Fin, Jamie was laid-back about things like that, not to mention pouring scorn on being overly PC; the two of us made a career of it. And while I hope we've grown up, I doubt Sanna has had a personality change. It's just basic respect.'

Now was the perfect time to tell him they had made contact, instead she swerved. 'I've often wondered how many adopted children get the birth parents they dream of, anyway.'

Fin laughed at that. 'When I was six I kept telling people mine were dinosaurs and at ten I'd've wanted them to be Jedi. Now, I just want . . .'

'A man?' Alina filled the pause. 'Fin, it's okay to feel that way—'

'No!' Fin rubbed the side of his head. 'You'd think that would be it, but it's not. Ali, I like the idea of Sanna being Sanna. It makes her, it makes me, *us* special. And I feel guilty for that, it seems off somehow.'

'We all want to be special, Fin, and we want to think our parents are special.' Alina considered it. 'It would be much worse if you wanted nothing to do with her because she is Sanna. Wouldn't it?'

'Suppose. Yes, of course it would. You make it sound simple, Ali.'

'Sometimes things are simple, Fin.' She sighed. And sometimes they were bloody, stupidly and unnecessarily complicated. She shook her head. 'A professor of *Peace Studies*, for God's sake.'

Fin laughed out loud. 'I can't believe that's the thing you're stuck on.'

'You never knew Jamie.'

In step, they circled the woodland walk towards the Botanic Cottage, and then went off-road slightly, no need to push through bare branches or delve deep into forestry. For a child, though, it had been the end point of an adventure trail, a real trek from the East Gate, and a puzzle to find. As adults, it was the symbol that rooted their relationship.

'There it is. Over there.' Fin pointed.

They stopped for a few seconds, both looking at their adopted tree.

'Do you remember—' and, 'I was just remembering—' emerged from their mouths at the same time, and they smiled.

'Ready?' Ali asked, and took his arm.

It was solid and unwavering, this spot they'd made their own. As she stepped off the path, Alina let out a breath; part of her thought it disappeared when they weren't there.

The Finally Tree.

Barely a day older in tree lore, benignly haggard, its roots spreading, growing, entangled with the smaller specimens around it.

Fin put his hand on the curved branch he'd first called a window. 'I could still climb through.'

'*You* could. I'm not trying.'

'Spoilsport.'

The Finally Tree had taken root when Fin turned

eleven. That autumn, gone was his fascination with pine cones and horse chestnuts. He was immersed in the fantasy world of elementals and root spirits, leading them to stray deep into the Woodland Garden, damp and deep in shadow. Later, in a tangle of ancient rhizomes and stems (his words) they had come upon a tree resembling a teapot, a long spout-like branch up high and on the other side, another curling back on itself to create a huge circle against the trunk.

'Ali, look, it's a window into another world,' he'd said, and she'd felt it too, for a second, the illusion of a curious mirror-land just beyond them. She'd shivered, but Fin had shattered the momentary melancholy with a delighted battle cry. He'd hoisted himself up, climbed through the hole and taunted her from the other side.

'Fin! I don't think that's allowed. And I'm too big,' she'd protested, but she hadn't been, not quite.

On a dry-enough bed of leaves, cushioned by jackets and hoods, they picked through the ritual jelly beans: all the green ones for him, the purple ones for her.

'This is our tree,' Fin had announced, mid-chew. 'Finders keepers. The Fin and Ali Tree.'

Soon it became the Fin-Ali Tree, and, ultimately, the Finally Tree.

It was there, one summer, when Fin had said, 'Ali, I think I'd like to search for Jamie. Mum and Dad are okay with it. How about you?'

What could she say? Jamie had been absent, a mystery, for over a decade and a half by then, but Fin had never been overly curious about that time; Alina had never had to tell him anything other than the truth. She crossed her fingers and gave her blessing. And when ten more years of Botanics meet-ups bore no news, it seemed that Jamie really had vanished.

'Tell me something about back then,' Fin said, nudging her. 'Go on, tell me a story, Ali. Like the old days.'

'All right . . . Well . . .' What had she not told him that she *could* tell him? 'It was here,' she said suddenly. 'Here in the Gardens, when I first told Jamie I was expecting you.'

1994

She hadn't meant to blurt it out in the middle of the gardens on a wet Wednesday evening. They were supposed to be going to the cinema in town, and then getting chips on the way home. She was late and Jamie leant on the stone wall just inside the main entrance, with his hands in his pockets. He'd looked fragile, hunched into his oversized waterproof coat, and she felt a rush of affection; inside he was a powerhouse. He'd know what to do.

'Where've you been?' he greeted her. 'I thought you weren't coming. Old ladies on a day trip keep stopping to talk to me and promising me my wee lassie will turn up. What's with this mysterious change of plan?'

Alina was silent, none of her rehearsed words came to the fore, and Jamie's eyes narrowed. 'Come on. What is it, Ally Bally? What've you been up to?'

'Getting pregnant,' she'd blurted. Yep, just like that; one thing she did remember clearly. The second thing was his face. He had known straight away she was serious – no fading smirk as the punchline wasn't forthcoming – but he hadn't looked shocked either, or said, 'Are you sure?' which were the only reactions she'd been contemplating. Instead he'd said, 'Oh, you poor thing, you must be out of your mind with worry. Come here,' and he'd gathered her up into his arms as well as the crinkly waterproof jacket would let him. She had begun to cry with big blotchy tears, and he let her. Standing right there, still, under a dripping bush.

After a few minutes she'd calmed down enough to be heaving sobs into his shoulder and realised the movie tickets were digging into her left eye. She took them out of his pocket and looked up. 'We're missing the film. Sorry,' she'd said.

'I don't think there's anything on that could have matched the drama of this,' he'd said. 'Come on, let's walk and talk about it. Then we'll go home and have . . . well, maybe not a bottle of wine, but some hot chocolate.'

The rest of the evening a blur. As Alina stood now, it was like looking down the wrong end of a telescope to view herself and Jamie cocooned in dampness – the drizzle must have gained momentum as they paced, running hand in hand to the gates when they were ready to be locked. On the bus – letting the windows steam up around them and then drinking hot chocolate that was not hot enough, sticky and cloying. They'd made a list. She frowned, she thought they'd made a list, but what was on it was a blur in time. Jamie had written down pregnancy test kit, she remembered that.

'I don't need one. I know,' she'd protested.

Then burst into tears again. Her panic had been less the

fear of pregnancy than the humiliation of it, she realised much later. She'd gone and done what everyone expected her to do; that would teach her to have university notions, they'd say. How could she have been so stupid to let the told-you-so brigade win, she'd wailed at Jamie. Her parents wouldn't be fussed – half of her school year had babies already – but they'd expect a ring, or a promise, at least.

'What the fuck do we care, Ally-Bally?' They were in his flat by then, Alina in his bed, Jamie tucking the covers up around her and stroking her forehead as if she had a fever. His voice sounded loud suddenly, and purposeful. 'We'll stand up to the lot of them.'

That *we* had made her cry some more.

'Are you sure you'll be all right if I go out and buy the test?' he asked her. 'I can go in the morning, instead. Though if you keep crying I'll have to go and get tissues anyway.' He squeezed her shoulder. 'It's not the end of the world, Alina, it's the beginning of a new one.'

That had made her laugh, hiccupping through her tears. 'Did you get that off the back of a cereal packet?'

'It was the blurb on a video game, I think. But don't knock it – crisis and opportunity are all the same thing, right? All right, stop groaning.' He'd jumped up, pulled his jacket back on and rummaged under the bed for his satchel. 'I'll stick to the practical and leave the self-help to your 'ology friends, who will really get off on being politically correct and understanding.'

Jamie's had been exactly the right tone to take with her; just as there was black humour in tragedy, so was there levity in gravity. She'd flapped him out of the door, then set herself to thinking logically. She didn't want a pregnancy test but she did want to be alone for a while. She had the worm of an idea, a clever, solve-everything idea, and she needed to work out how to sell it to Jamie.

FRIDAY

And sell it she had, eventually, though she had never been exactly sure why he agreed. The pregnancy test was the spectre at the feast, Alina's days and nights filled with a taunting chant: *Take the test, take the test.* 'I can't,' she'd eventually screamed at Jamie, when he discovered her with her hands over her ears to block the noise. 'If I do, I can't ever pretend again that nothing had happened that night.' He said nothing, just held her, and soon after that, he agreed to her plan.

Now, she could ask him why, she thought, as D-day dawned, and she was entering, again, the East Gate of the Botanics. She wondered if anyone noticed her, back yet again, a succession of different meetings in different places, and usually with a big umbrella, just in case. She could be high-end, taking out the enemy with a clever prick of a needle, or doing a common-or-garden drugs drop. Truth was, Alina had never had a garden of her own, knew nothing about horticulture, she'd always treated the Botanics as a grand backyard, slipping in and out at will – but three times in a week was unusual.

Alina and Jamie had always meandered, weather-dependent, gravitating towards the rock garden. If she ever tied the knot, it was going to be there, she told herself, relaxed amongst the redwoods, with a barbecue close by and back-up from the Caledonian Hall when the Scottish summer got too much. In the meantime, Alina sat where she'd get her first glimpse of Sanna, where she'd have time to settle the right look on her face.

She counted her heartbeats with the seconds. One . . . Two . . . Three . . . It was turning into a nice day, great for strolling, maybe less so for sitting out; the strategically placed benches were empty, just a lone brief-cased figure, leaning heavily on a walking stick, and a cluster of Japanese students taking photographs. Not even in the most hectic of imaginations could any of them be Sanna. Forty-six . . . Forty-seven . . . Forty-eight . . .

Wait. Alina tensed. A woman hampered by flat but broad cardboard box, casual in red Converse trainers and a cream raincoat, looking around as if lost. Alina squinted, stood up and took a step forward, just as the other woman looked directly at her and did the same. They walked towards each other, pace for pace and part of Alina wanted to laugh; all that was missing was the Glienicke Bridge.

It was a certain familiarity in the woman's gait, the way her right hand was in the pocket of her mac and the angle at which a satchel was slung over the same shoulder. Jamie had walked exactly like that – it's what she'd seen in Fin, too – and he'd had an Indiana Jones satchel long before Joey from Friends hit on the man-bag. The flash of déjà vu was infinitesimal but sufficient; this *was* Sanna coming towards her, and looking as uncertain as Alina felt.

Alina swallowed. 'Sanna?'

'Alina.'

Slowly, Alina put out a hand across the no-man's land between them, and Sanna reached out to take it. The firm grip held for a second, then one of them – Alina was never sure afterwards who – gave a strangulated giggle, and somehow they were enveloped in a hug. An awkward hug, Alina thought, but nowhere near as awkward as a quarter of a century, an adopted child, a gender transition – and a flat cardboard box (*I hope that's not a cake, or it's done for*, flew through her mind) – might have been.

Then they just stood and looked at each other. Sanna's frame was as slight as it had ever been, her hair shoulder length and darker, highlighted, her teeth – Alina had so coveted those white, straight teeth – still perfect. The glasses – dark, angular frames – were new; Jamie hadn't worn glasses, but they highlighted Sanna's brown eyes and defined cheekbones. Alina wondered briefly how she bore up: still shortish, still plumpish, darkish skin and darker-than-Sanna brown eyes; Alina had always been very *ish*.

'So, what do you think?' It was Sanna who spoke first. She held her arms out wide, then gestured head to toe. 'Would you have recognised me?' She smiled, a shadow of Jamie's smile, but it didn't hide the anxiety in her voice.

'You . . . you . . .' It was on the tip of Alina's tongue to say, *you haven't changed a bit*, but she winced at how insulting, downright *hurtful* that might sound if there'd been too much water under the bridge. 'I recognised your walk.' Alina tempered it. 'And your smile. Oh, and the satchel, except you've upgraded cotton for leather.'

They smiled, the bubble of relief almost palpable.

Then Sanna pointed down and grinned. 'Red shoes.'

'Snap.' Alina put one foot forward. 'Do you think life

might have been different if we hadn't both worn red shoes that day?'

'No. You still would have been the only one who didn't scare the shit out of me in the cross-dressing class.'

'We thought we were so clever calling it that, didn't we?'

'We thought we were clever full stop.'

There was silence again, then Sanna gestured to the bench. 'Now we've established neither of us is going to bolt straightaway, shall we sit down?'

They sat.

'Where have you come from?' Alina asked.

'Bradford. I work at the university. And you? You live in Edinburgh, right?'

'Half the year. The other half I run an orphanage in Dhaka, in Bangladesh.'

'Wow. You ran away even further than I did.' Sanna hesitated. 'Sorry, I shouldn't assume—'

'No, you're right. It's a long story though.'

'I think we've both got those.'

'Yes.'

They smiled at each other and the conversation lapsed, but it wasn't blind date awkward; more, Alina thought, like the few minutes familiarisation when you settle into a different model of car to drive. After a solicitous few minutes remarking on the weather and asking each other if they were warm enough, comfortable, wanted a drink, would rather go into the café . . . there was nothing else left to share, and Sanna finally said, 'Hark at us. Shades of what we used to be. The wee wifeys we used to mimic saying *I told you so*.'

'God, we were mean, weren't we.'

'We were kids.'

It's going to be all right, Alina told herself. It's going to be all right. But it was the past that was all right, really, the present was so big that she actually had no idea where to start. The twenty-five unknown years hung like a yawning fathomless canyon between them. Trembling, she wrapped her hands in her scarf, gripping it like a safety rope. The sudden urge to run was almost overwhelming.

'Don't.' Sanna reached over and put her hand over Alina's balled fists. 'You're not the one who runs away, Alina. I am. I did. But not anymore.'

Alina was silent. Fighting. She closed her eyes. Every six months she was still running; but Sanna didn't know that, did she?

'We've done the hardest bit,' Sanna persisted, and with her eyes closed Alina heard Jamie's voice. 'We're here. If that's all we manage today, it's enough.'

She was right, of course she was right. Alina had to hold this together for Fin's sake, if nothing else.

'So . . . what do you really think? Be truthful.' Sanna indicated the length of her body. 'Come on. Spit it out. Two decades of heartache. Wondering, hoping, hiding. Of hormones and outrageous surgical procedures.' Her voice was droll; nervous eye tic invisible if you didn't know her. 'Ally-Bally, was it worth it?'

I won't ever change, Ally-Bally. Alina had to get this right. She had to. 'Sanna Andrews,' she dared, finally. 'You haven't changed a bit.'

Five seconds and about a hundred years passed. Alina, unable to tell whether Sanna remembered that long ago pact or not, could have ruined everything. Then:

'Fabulous.' Sanna's rapidly blinking eyes twinkled. 'And, thanks. I think.' Then, quietly, 'I remember what I promised,' she added.

Alina sighed. 'I remember you saved me.'

'We saved each other.' Sanna nodded. 'Seriously, Alina, if it wasn't for you, I don't think I . . . I mean, *I Sanna*, would be here today.' She looked up and caught Alina's eye. 'But hey, we can spend the *next* twenty-five years musing on all that.'

When Alina didn't respond, Sanna went on, nodding slowly. 'Ah, yes. The real elephant in the room.' She said it as Alina thought it. That had always been their way. 'I'm assuming nothing's changed?' she asked. 'That you still don't know for sure − whether Fin *is* my son?'

Alina winced, it sounded so stark. Then she felt Sanna's hand on hers again. Alina turned to look at her. 'No,' she said, her breath hitched, 'Sanna, I don't know.'

1994

Alina's plan was so far from logical it verged on the insane, but once she'd hit on it, everything fell into place. Twenty-five years on, with the results of that decision hitting her head-on like a train crash, Alina wondered again (and *again*) how she could ever have played with so many lives. But she hadn't been looking at the future, had she, just for an acceptable, immediate solution; her idea of the wider picture had been putting a frame around the pregnancy and legitimising it.

Jamie had been gone ages that night. She used the time alternately to fret, and to plan. It all hinged on him; depended whether his idea of support even went as far as holding her hand in an abortion clinic or in the delivery room, because what she was asking went much further.

When he did get back, a good couple of hours later, she was wrapped in his duvet and staring at the screen of the black and white portable TV, which was very modest for someone who knew so much about computers.

'I had to go halfway around the world,' he complained. 'Who would have thought it so bloody hard to find a late-night chemist?'

Alina sat up and hugged her knees, wondering how to tell him he needn't have bothered.

He rummaged in the satchel and brandished a paper bag. 'One pregnancy test as recommended by the pharmacist himself, and a big box of tissues just in case.'

'You're very brave.' Alina meant it. 'I'd have skulked and snatched.'

'Which is why you sent me.' Jamie handed over the bag. 'You do look a zillion times better than when I left.'

'My head's clearer now.' Alina hesitated, still holding the pharmacy bag, and Jamie had misread it. 'Do you want me to go out again while you do it? Or read the instructions to you?' he asked.

Alina shook her head and got up slowly, placing the unopened bag on his desk. 'It says it's best to do the test in the morning, but Jamie . . . I've got an idea.' She leant against the desk and watched him take off his jacket and hang it up on the back of the door. He kicked off his trainers and pushed them, with the side of his foot, to jumble with hers at a spot near the door. Then he sat down on the bed and looked up at her.

'Go on, then,' he said.

She stood there, dumb, not realising she was twirling at a loose thread until it bit into her finger and cut off the circulation. 'Ouch.' She unwound it and sucked her finger. 'I don't know how to ask you,' she said at last.

'Okay.' Jamie's glance didn't falter. 'Well, I can't think of anything you can't ask me. I'm tougher than I look, you know. Although,' he added, and she wasn't sure if he was being serious, 'I'm not sure I'm tough enough to go and give your one-night stand a good thumping, if that's on your mind?'

'No, of course, it's not. I don't know who . . . I mean I don't want him to know . . .' Alina was distracted, flustered.

'What is it, Ally-Bally? Tell me.' He put his hand on her cheek and turned her to face him. 'Alina, whatever it is, I'll do it. I love you. You're the best friend I've ever had.' He swallowed. 'You've made such a difference to me.'

'I have? How?' She was surprised, adding a slightly belated, 'I love you, too, Jamie.'

He shook his head. 'Not now, Alina Dowd. This is your crisis time. Come on, what's your solution?'

'I thought, well, I thought . . . Look, I'm pregnant, Jamie, I'm sure of it, I don't need the test. But maybe there's a tiny chance I might not be.' There was nothing like contradicting yourself in the same breath. She searched Jamie's face but it didn't change, he actually looked as if he might understand. 'I can't face an abortion. And I can't keep a baby, it's just not the right time.' She stopped, making sure Jamie was with her.

'Then you're talking about having a baby and having it adopted?'

'Yes. Exactly.' She looked at him hopefully.

'But?' Jamie took her hand. 'Don't look at me like that, Ally-Bally. There's a huge screaming 'but' at the end of that sentence.'

She was quaking, when the realisation started to cross his face, but he didn't let go of her hand so that had to be a good sign.

'You want me to pretend to be the baby's father, don't you?' he said.

Alina blinked, fitting in a momentary prayer to an all-understanding, all-forgiving God she didn't believe in. 'Yes. But,' she plunged on, now or never, 'but we could make it so it wasn't really a lie. I mean if we slept together a few times, had sex,' *Jesus, Alina, he knows what sex is*, 'the baby could be yours. Technically.' She stopped. Did it still sound plausible out loud?

'Technically,' Jamie repeated. 'Like the National Lottery? Or a game of Russian Roulette?'

She listened for sarcasm, but his tone was neutral. In hindsight, she came to admire that immense show of self-control. He was nineteen, had a pregnancy dumped on him, gone out and made small talk with a pharmacist over a pregnancy test, and then was hit with *that*; Alina's idea of the century. He really had loved her, she thought.

The next minute, though, it all crashed around her.

He still hadn't let go of her hand, in fact he'd tightened his grasp.

'Alina Dowd,' he'd said, 'Are you *completely* fucking insane?'

FRIDAY

For a second, Alina thought, it was as if they were both reliving it, time and place distorted in the swirl of memories. The figure in the glass turned then, and she felt a sudden jolt as Jamie became Sanna once more.

'I realised a lot about me over those few months,' Sanna said. 'Oh, there was no great epiphany, I didn't jump off the 42 bus with a "Hallelujah, I'm a woman trapped in a man's body", but somewhere – and if it gets wacky and into your social-workerish zone, then sue me – it began to occur to me that you weren't just a woman I admired, you were the woman I wanted to be.' She shrugged, a self-conscious mix of defiance and embarrassment. 'That night, I came back all fired up to be your best friend, your birth partner, the baby's godparent, whatever.'

'And you got whatever with a capital W.' Alina smiled faintly, even as the tears prickled her eyes.

'I did – but then again, being asked to father a baby was the best distraction ever, wasn't it?' She looked down at her hands. 'So there you have it, Alina Dowd. That's why I agreed to your totally insane idea. Whoever had said the past was another country was wrong, it was another fucking continent.'

Alina folded herself into Sanna's hug. It was weird, that twenty-five years on, their bodies moulded into a familiar position, head against shoulder, arms tightening . . . Despite herself, Alina stiffened suddenly, and Sanna's voice, muffled in her hair, sounded amused.

'You've just noticed the difference, haven't you?' she said. She pulled back slightly and glanced down at the modest swell of breasts under her loose sweater. 'Don't worry, it still surprises me sometimes.'

They looked at each other and began to giggle, far more than was warranted.

Insane or not, Alina's plan had worked out exactly. She had set up a schedule, 'A nought to sixty in ten days fuck-fest,' Jamie called it. He likened their coupling to doggedly eating their way through a nice enough Christmas dinner, even though neither really fancied it and they wouldn't have bothered if left to themselves. All that had mattered was they had done it enough to lay favourable odds – in a totally illogical way but well enough to suit anyone who didn't know the order of events – of Jamie being the baby's father.

'So Fin knows nothing about any of this? I don't mean the crazy detail, but the fact that his birth father might be a nameless one-night stand?'

'Ouch. No, he knows nothing. Sanna, I spent so much time convincing myself that you were definitely the baby's . . . other parent that I believed it utterly. I had a jitter when he said he wanted to find you, but it was literally when I got his text saying he had, that it all imploded. What I did was, well, *bizarre* is the word I keep coming back to.'

'What *we* did.' Sanna shrugged. 'Could have, should have, would have. We faced it then and we'll face it now. The question is, how?'

It was now or never, a stark choice: pretend Sanna was who Fin thought she was and live with the deception for another twenty-five (or fifty, or more) years, or tell Fin the truth and have him live with their lie. Oh yes, they could discover the objective truth with a DNA test, but that was its own quagmire. If that didn't match Jamie's, then Fin would never find his birth father because Alina couldn't identify him in a line-up of lookalikes. And if it did, that meant he was deliberately conceived – unnecessarily – to mask an accident that had never happened.

Alina's head swam with the Hobson's Choice her teenage self had created. 'Toss a bloody coin?' she said eventually.

Sanna spoke slowly, then, as if she was working something out, 'If we were in the same situation now – would you do the pregnancy test?'

'It's the first thing I'd do.'

'Well, we can't go back and change the people we were, nor what we did. But we're different people now and would do something very different so . . .' Sanna raised one eyebrow.

'So we should come clean?'

'Do you think Fin would want to know?'

Alina laughed. 'That's the stupid thing, Jamie. Fin's all about truth, and forgiveness, too. I've never been worried he wouldn't forgive me, I'm just so ashamed I've put *my son* in that position.'

'Our son.'

'*Our* son, yes. That's it.' Alina blinked through tears. 'You're more his parent than anyone else, biological or not. You were there from the beginning, you and I made the big decisions, bizarre or not. The three of us were a family for a little while. A five minute drunken shag doesn't compete.'

'It does mean Fin loses his Get Out of Jail Free card though,' Sanna said. 'You know what I mean,' she went on, in a faux drawl, '"Meet my dad, y'all, the tranny-Annie". For a lot of people that would be far worse than the drunken shag.'

'Not Fin.' Alina shook her head. 'And you're not, I mean—' Her eyes widened. 'Oh my God, I called you Jamie, didn't I? I'm sorry. I'm so sorry . . .'

Sanna let her run on a downward spiral, before saying, 'Alina, do shut up. You've called me worse. We've both called other people worse.' She tapped on the cardboard box she'd left on the bench beside her. 'I brought this, in case of awkward moments and I can see you think this is one.'

Alina grabbed the lifeline. 'What is it?'

'It's our project, remember? The sociology and statistics thing we had to partner up for. It's dire – we were too taken up with Fin, our real project. Take it home, have a look. There's a few photos at the back, even some baby ones I scanned and printed.'

'Why don't you email those to Fin?' Alina suggested. 'Easy way to make contact? He can send some of himself to you, too.'

'Brilliant idea.'

Alina leaned back and stretched out her legs. 'Do you

know, it might have been the jet lag or wishful thinking but on Monday, he really reminded me of you, his walk, and that thing you do with your eyebrow.'

'Ding ding,' said Sanna. 'That and the 10 to 1 ratio of sex sessions in my favour.'

'Ah, but eye colour's still the sticking point. Two browns making a blue – possible. Not probable.'

'Well, whatever the science,' Sanna said, 'look at us, Ally-Bally, is any of this situation probable?'

'True enough.' Alina changed tack. 'We meet here a lot when I'm home, Fin and me. History repeating itself. When he was little, we found a secret magic tree that we called the Finally Tree.' Alina smiled. 'Fin can tell you why. It's not actually secret or magic, it's a Dunkeld Larch. We even adopted it.'

'Go, you and Fin. Can I meet this family tree?'

'You must,' Alina said. 'It's a European and Japanese hybrid. The geographically separated parent species were brought together specially to create it . . . You could read a message into that, couldn't you?' Alina grinned. 'But don't look impressed because that's all I remember.'

'Does that make Fin the gardener? What *does* he do?' Sanna asked. 'Please tell me he's something solid – a plumber or a nurse?'

'He's training to be a Salvation Army officer.'

'Well, that's something I wouldn't have guessed. I never thought I'd have a son in the church.'

'I never thought he'd have a parent as a professor. Of Peace Studies,' Alina said, sliding her eyes sideways.

'Touché, Ally-Bally. Ah, well, it shows you can choose

your family, but you've no control over who they turn out to be,' Sanna said, wisely.

'Well, he said you sounded interesting, and he likes interesting.'

'Good.' Sanna stood up and rubbed the bottom of her back. 'He won't complain, then, will he? When he gets it in spades from us . . . Be careful what you wish for, as they say.'

SATURDAY

'I've met her, Fin, but . . .'

Alina was tempted to send the text like that but thought better of it. Yesterday's reunion might have been uncommonly fairy-tale-like − she was riding on that repeated *we*: Sanna upholding Jamie's promise − but it was too soon to promise happy ever after.

She picked up the phone instead and made a WhatsApp call.

'I've met her, Fin. I met Sanna. Yesterday—'

'Ali? You've met her already?' He interrupted, eyes wide. 'What's she like? Is she like Jamie was? I mean, did you remember her? Have you got any photos?'

'She said she would send you some pictures, check your emails.'

'Really? I'll look right now. Keep talking, though, Ali.'

Fin's excitement was infectious, like the once-little boy under the Finally Tree, and Alina took a deep breath. 'She really wants to see you. She's exactly like the person I remember,' Alina was struggling to explain, 'except she's female. I don't know if that makes sense? I told her she hadn't changed a bit.'

'You did *what*?' Fin's face turned back to the phone screen, his grin becoming first incredulous then impressed. 'Seriously, Ali, if you said that and it's still all good, then she ... you ... Well, you must have had something special.'

'We did. We have.' Alina pulled a face to hide her emotion, and indicated Fin himself.

'Aw, Ali. I can't believe you've met her.'

'I've met her, Fin, but—'

There was a bang on the door in the background and Fin disappeared. 'Hold that thought, Ali. Hermes delivery, gotta grab him.'

Crap. Maybe it was a sign that WhatsApp wasn't the place to announce more *buts*. Sitting in no-man's land, Alina sent Sanna a text: *I'm on to Fin now. Standby.* But Fin was gone so long, Alina got fidgety and hung up, wondering what on earth he was getting delivered.

Sanna replied in the meantime: *I sent him some photos and he's just sent some back (no messages, just a name and a kiss). I'm about to open them ...*

'Am I the only one out of the picture party?' Alina murmured to herself, before remembering the hard copies in the cardboard box. She put the laminated spiral project carefully to one side and pulled out a thin envelope of what she assumed were the photos.

Before she could open them, her phone rang and pinged a notification virtually simultaneously. She clicked on WhatsApp and Fin came to life on the screen, saying, 'Wait til you see this, Ali,' just as Sanna's text message flashed across the top: *You need to see this.*

What? What was the fuss? Alina was irritated suddenly. What was she, air traffic control? After a minute of faffing and juggling with screens and attachments and links, not to mention carrying on two conversations at once over different media, Alina's nerves were at breaking point. She gave up and terminated both; she'd blame the internet connection later.

As mood swings went, it was colossal, she'd have called it a panic attack if she was prone to them. She went into the kitchen to make some tea, changed her mind and poured a glass of red wine, which she sipped, leaning on the ledge of the open window. The cold air and scurrying clouds soothed her. She was allowed to be out of sorts, she'd been on a twenty-five-year-and-six-day collision course, gaining such final momentum that she was hurtling the last hundred yards—

To the start.

With a sense of fatalism, she sat back down at her computer, she looked, casually enough, at the images Fin and Sanna had shared and then, scanning the images like a forensic scientist, she viewed them again.

The camera didn't lie, did it. Not an old Polaroid, anyway, that couldn't be Photoshopped to tell a whopper.

Fin, on the right, and Jamie, on the left, were like twins in a spot-the-difference puzzle. It wasn't just a case of all babies looking similar, if one of them had been superimposed onto the other background, they'd look like identical twins. Even in totally different outfits, one on a sheepskin rug clutching a knitted sheep, the other with a plastic ball, one in sunshine, one in shadow. The way they sat, legs slightly bent, and splayed for balance, their chubby knees exposed, and that left eyebrow quizzically raised as if to say, 'Another photo? Really?' Their colouring, their features, even the sticking up strands of hair at the crown, were the same.

If only we'd stayed in touch, Alina thought – and then dismissed it. Yes, they would have seen the likenesses sooner, worried about those bright eye colours, the brown and the blue, being the – possible not probable – anomaly. But would they really have told a younger Fin about their bizarre pact? Really?

When Fin called back later, Alina was ready for him, but his euphoria was cut through with a frown.

'Ali,' he said, 'I got carried away. Before we saw the photos, you were saying something and I cut you off. You said you'd met Sanna *but*—'

'But,' Alina intervened, improvising swiftly, 'she wants to meet you at the Finally Tree, and to do it before this coronavirus takes hold of us and adds another year to the missing twenty-five. She wants – we both want – *finally* to tell you the story of us.'

In Loving Memory

2011–2021, Rosebank Cemetery

NADINE AISHA JASSAT

The summer before I moved to Scotland, and almost a year before I made Edinburgh my home, I came on a family trip to see the city. It was late July, the weekend that turning point I now know so well: the city poised halfway between the regular hum of its residents, and the excited surge of visitors for the August festivals soon to come. It feels fitting, looking back, that I arrived at this time: a time of in-betweens, of transition between the city embodying *home* and tipping into *discovery*. Anything can happen in these crossover spaces where one thing becomes another: sunset or sunrise, doorways and arches, eighteenth birthdays, and Edinburgh's last weekend in July.

We came: my father, my mother, my auntie, and I. All spring previously, I had been in Zimbabwe with Auntie, Harare's autumn turning into winter by the time I crossed the equator – another in-between so present in my life – and came back to this small isle. An approved visa application later, and Auntie followed – just in time to witness the late summer heat, so rare in Britain that we never know if we are going to get it at all. We decided to go to Scotland for the weekend, since we knew that I was about to move there. The university I was to be studying at for a year was the alma mater of a famous prince, and as we drove up in the car Auntie made jokes in her sing-song voice about how maybe I would find one, and earn my crown. I laughed, but as I sat there – my fingers running along the glass edge of my open window, hair dancing about my face as we zoomed along the motorway towards the border – I thought about how I didn't want to find a prince so much as freedom. So much as a fresh start, a life to call my own. I think maybe I even felt it, the hum of it beginning, as we crossed the border and I squinted at my reflection in the wing mirror. A sense of crossing over; a sense of beginning anew.

That summer, even the air itself was hot. It pressed against my face, running in dry breaths down my throat and nose, as the hairs at the nape of my neck curled and my body expanded, trying to get used to the sensation of sweat. I remember getting on the bus with Auntie, relieved when I saw the fabric seats and not a plastic faux leather my skin would be sure to stick to. Auntie commented with excited glee on people's accents and I felt shy that they could hear, but everybody just went about their days in that Edinburgh way I've become accustomed to. She felt such joy in being in a new place and I suppose I did, too. We walked along the castle walls and took a photo by an old navy-blue police phone box – her still wrapped in her mackintosh, me in an embroidered cotton kurta she'd given me, the metallic strands of embroidery twirling off with the lightest of contact, leaving bits of gold on me and on the fabric bus seats. I was already planting myself here – all sparks of gold and twirled threads. I was already leaving a trail.

We'd rented a flat for the week in a sandy-yellow apartment complex. It was a large modern two-bed, its back windows overlooking a graveyard I now know to be Rosebank Cemetery. The cemetery was bordered by a stone wall that we had passed when we drove up to the rented flat, and the wall was high enough that it wasn't until I got to the bedroom that I saw the cemetery behind it, and how close to it we would be sleeping. Looking out, I could see rows of grey headstones spaced out among green grass and slightly lighter, uneven paths. Perhaps there were even trees, but I don't remember that so much – I just remember the grey stones, and the sense of it being a familiar sight. I had grown up in Yorkshire, and graveyards were not far away sites of remembrance held at a distance, but clusters both holy and familiar that rose up in churchyards around every other corner. We'd made school trips to them with the art teacher, who would instruct us to set paper and pencil over the headstones and make etchings of their marks. So, looking out at Rosebank, its proximity did not bother me. If anything, my moment's pause at the bedroom window, before I turned to unpack my bags, was more a nod of recognition, an acknowledgement of its presence. A hello.

That night, we dressed for an evening's adventure in the city. My father had promised, if not insisted upon, a trip to Kebab Mahal, a tiny Indian restaurant, which he had returned to for years ever since his first visit to Edinburgh when I was a child. The restaurant has expanded now, but back then it was a small and narrow café tucked away near Edinburgh's Central Mosque. It had a glass counter at the entrance filled with the treats of my childhood dreams: not just savoury eats like samoosas, but also jalebis, gulab jamun, rasmalai. The four of us packed around a small table, shoulder to shoulder we ate, meeting hand straight to mouth, roti wrapped around mutton or veg, tongue meeting spice. I leaned back my head and sighed at the rich flavours, the dishes not changed to meet the tastes of someone else, but real and true to themselves, true cooking found in the heart of Edinburgh. Afterwards, while my parents paid and chatted to the owner, Auntie and I eased ourselves out, both holding on to our bellies as if they were so full we needed our hands to help us carry them. We went into the grocery store next door, Auntie ooh-ing and aah-ing at this and that, and comparing what we could find here to what she could get back in Zimbabwe.

'Amla!' She exclaimed, when we reached the beauty section, tinned pulses to our left and cordials and juice to our right. She grabbed a box from the shelf, on the front of it a picture of a woman with long, dark hair, white flowers flowing through it. Inside it was a bottle of what Auntie promised would be fantastic hair oil – *'used by all the girls in India!'* – that would be a welcome addition to my current regime, which she'd also taught me, of steeping bottles of solid coconut oil in hot water, before combing the hot liquid through my hair and letting it soak overnight. The Amla oil, made from gooseberries, was blended with jasmine, which Auntie assured me would offset what was an otherwise quite powerful smell. We bought it, a small £2.99 for a bottle sure to last months, and left.

Later on, back in our rented flat in Pilrig Heights, I sat at Auntie's feet as my parents chatted over the TV, and she ran the oil through my hair. Her fingers moved from my scalp to my hair's ends and back again, digging and swirling and rubbing the Amla in. The scent of jasmine undercut by something else, something stronger and sharper, almost cloying, ran through the flat, and my mother insisted on me sleeping on a towel so not to stain the pillowcases. The heat had climbed significantly at this point, all of our bodies gleaming as if covered in the same jasmine oil that wound itself round my head, my mother and I fanning ourselves, the former wondering how she was going to sleep as the thermometer hovered dangerously close to thirty degrees. Proclaiming himself 'a man of action', my father set up a fan in each of our rooms before we went to bed; my parents in the master, and my aunt and I sharing two single beds in the second, smaller room.

As we got into bed, I switched the fan on and closed the open window, briefly glimpsing Rosebank Cemetery's grey headstones and memorial monuments, winking grey in the dark. I lay down with only a single sheet covering me, my body spread wide, as Auntie and I joked that we looked like starfish lying together in our twin beds as we stared at the ceiling. The fan rotated steadily, blowing currents of air, which moved like invisible hands along the sheets, the smell of jasmine and Amla circling with each blast.

I closed my eyes, Auntie's breathing settling into a rhythm beside me, the fan humming round. *Breath. Fan. Hum. Breath. Fan. Hum.* The world became a distant place of heat and that same rhythm, as I crossed from being awake into a hazy in-between, sinking down into sleep.

Time passed, eyes moving behind closed lids, bodies curled into their sleep shapes. Still the rhythm continued: *breath, fan, hum,* circling around and around.

And I slept. Solidly. Soundly. Dark behind eyelids, restful mind, I slept.

Until – whispering.

Tugging just there at the edge of my consciousness, like

one of those gold strands left on the bus was still clinging to me, calling me back.

Whisper-whisper-whisper.

My mind turned slightly, face frowning, as I rolled over, willing whoever it was to be quiet.

Whisper-whisper-whisper.

Groggy and pulled out of sleep, I inched open my eyes to identify the cause of the sound.

Whisper-whisper-whisper.

Eyes met haze and there, stood at the end of the bed, the silhouette of a man – hands cupped as if praying in the Islamic way – stood by my feet.

Whisper-whisper-whisper.

Dream and reality blurred, my head spinning and heart pounding. Was it my dad? The visitor had brown skin but his face – it was older than Dad, it was too old to be him. I squinted again: was it Uncle Ebrahim – but what would he be doing here? He was supposed to be in Zimbabwe. I took in the figure's stance, his lowered head, and had a vague notion that something in his outfit reminded me of the grocery store we had just visited, but that this was older too, more 1940s than now. My thoughts drew together, became more solid lines as I felt my body more awake, and yet the old uncle stayed. His face was concentrated as he prayed over my feet – and I realised with each shaking, chasing beat of my heart, with each second increasing its pace that no, it wasn't Uncle Ebrahim, it wasn't Dad, it was someone else.

Ghost, my instincts whispered, *ghost*.

Blood rushed in my ears, movement returning to my limbs, as I paused in that last split second between sleep and waking, heart chasing itself with adrenaline, face fixed on the apparition at the end of the bed. His single, solid form, continued on – hands cupped and head lowered as he stood over my feet, whispering, praying, speaking words over me.

Fear took over: I sat up sharply, kicked fully out of sleep as my body flipped vertical with panic. *Ghost-ghost-ghost-ghost-GHOST!* I took one last look at the figure standing, definitely standing, the man definitely there at the end of my bed, definitely whispering words over my feet – and I screamed. As if instinct was all that was left to me, as if the noise of my own voice was some kind of protection or call to arms, I screamed. Lungs and tongue and open mouth charging around the house, giving my fear noise, my emotion jumping into sound, I screamed.

Within moments, the lights were on – Dad rushing in, all pyjama-ed and panicked, Auntie sitting up in the bed next to me, her own voice alarmed: 'What's wrong, what's wrong, what's happening?'

'Ghost, ghost, ghost,' I stammered, my breath rising and falling in pants, my heart a reminder of life against my chest. 'There was a ghost praying over me, an old Indian man, he was dressed like a grocer – ghost, there was a ghost.'

My father shook his head in disbelief and almost disappointment at my dramatics, while Auntie cut in: 'Are you sure? Was it a djinn? Or maybe I think just a bad dream? I didn't see anything?'

'No, no, no – it was a ghost, there was a ghost stood at the end of my bed, he was here, I can't sleep here – there was a ghost!' I pointed a shaking finger to the empty space by my feet where the uncle had stood.

My father and Auntie looked at it, and then each other, as if conferring what best to do.

'Nadine,' my Dad said, 'it's two in the morning. Just go back to sleep. It's just a bad dream.'

'It wasn't a dream!'

'Well, there's nowhere else you can sleep, so either stay up in the dark paranoid or go back to sleep and accept it was a bad dream,' my father turned to the door, 'as I am going to bed.'

I shook my head repeatedly. 'I'm not sleeping in here, there was a ghost and he was whispering *exactly* over me, he had his hands cupped exactly over my feet!'

My father and Auntie looked at me, the first exasperated, the other hesitant, as if tempted by the supernatural, while also very tired and wishing for her pillow. I looked around me, wanting to look for something else to prove it to them, some other way of showing them that my testimony was real. And that was when I noticed it, another presence in the room. Pressing on my skin, with all the power of the former heat of the day, pressing against my father's crossed arms and Auntie's raised blanket. Wrapping around all of us, that last lingering presence left by the ghost.

In that space that had once been filled with the heat of a record-breaking July, the same room we'd struggled to sleep in, starfish tossing and turning upon the air's hot sea. That same air was changed. That same room was freezing, freezing cold.

I looked to my father and Auntie once more, and saw them take it in, too. 'You see,' I said. 'Ghost.'

The tale of Old Uncle Ghost followed me when I moved to Edinburgh a year later in 2012. Dad still insisted that the cold in the room was from the fan, and that the visitation was a dream concocted from the combination of too much food, glimpses of Rosebank Cemetery, and the invasive, all-encompassing scent of the Amla oil. I remained convinced of one thing: that I had crossed that border between asleep and awake, and was no longer dreaming by the time I sat up in bed screaming. That as I did so, my old ghost visitor, for a pause measuring a handful of heartbeats, had stayed. Had been with me in that in-between place.

Soon, that same city which had seemed so unfamiliar to me – the same buses that Auntie and I had climbed on to with excitement at the novelty, the same streets we'd gotten lost around – began to become home. By the end of my first year, I knew Leith so well I could draw you a map of it with my eyes closed – a map of it in my dreams – sleep whispered thoughts dancing down Leith Walk, or along the side streets which run off it like branches connecting it to the city's wider forest: Albert, Iona, Dalmeny.

I rented my first flat off one of these streets, a small one-bed off Albert Street, and though I didn't know it at the time, if you look at it on a map, it is almost exactly in a mirror position to that flat off Pilrig Street and Rosebank Cemetery, as if Leith Walk were the main line, and the two flats were balanced on either side. And whether that line represented the boundary between the past and the present, or the everyday and the supernatural, I do not know. However, I do know that something in me never ventured down to Pilrig Street, and always instead kept to the east side of the walk, away from the cemetery, and the past, and the ghost.

I was in my early twenties then, and working in my first job, for a cause I believed in, making my way through that transition between leaving my parents' home and finding and making my own. I had an idea in my head of all the things I wanted to be, wrote them on a cheap chalkboard that I displayed in my room: *articulate, in love, working for a cause that matters to me.* Even years later, after those dreams had morphed or changed, I could see the faint outline of the white on the board where I had first written them – as if, once wished out, their memory stayed.

I learned the ways you make a place home, and I learned them unintentionally, and on my own. There was the Sicilian pastry shop on the corner of Albert Street, where I would go to buy cartoccis: rectangular doughnuts shaped like swirled seashell horns and filled with vanilla custard, topped with a sugar sprinkling that stuck to your fingers, so that after you ate it you still had some sweetness to lick. There were the local charity shops on Leith Walk, the ones from which I bought both the clothes I wore and the furniture in my small flat. At some point over the years, hearts were painted on the pavement, their proclamations of love for Leith echoing what I felt inside me. On Saturdays, I would walk to Edinburgh's Royal Botanic Gardens via McDonald Road Library, on a winding path through side streets passing the muralled walls of Annandale Mosque, then a school playground, then grand Georgian homes. Later, I would go directly up Leith Walk, passing Waverley to join the Royal Mile and a small venue that was tucked away there, where I read my poems out loud for the first time.

With every step or turn of a street corner, every foot crossing over cobble or pavement or grass, I walked myself into knowing the city, and the city in turn walked itself into me: love for it filling me up with every purple sky over the clock face of the Balmoral Hotel, every clear day looking down to the sea from the golden cobbles of the Royal Mile, every after-work walk returning down that long tree trunk of Leith alive with people, with Aunties tossing dupattas over shoulders, socks tucked into flip-flops and Puffa jackets over kurtas, with the shop owner on the end of my street who would always wave as I passed by, with the inexplicable city seagulls, with fire engines, with life. Even the digital advertising billboard, a giant screen in the middle of Leith Walk, became a part of my daily landscape, and a distraction from the nearby building works which are now fancy apartments, but which I can still remember as an empty space of sky zig-zagged with cranes.

The city may have changed, but in my memory it lives in all its phases, as if time is only layers, which the mind can so easily move through and find again. This city is a place where time is not a fixed thing, but something that can be pulled back, pulled over, and moved through – light as thin cotton curtains in the wind, or whispered prayers spoken near midnight by a well-wishing ghost. Just as the modern apartment block overlooked the old headstones of Rosebank Cemetery, so too does the rest of the city, old and new sitting alongside each other. With each day, week and year that has passed in my decade in this city, Edinburgh has wrapped itself around my memory. I have made my life in it, and in doing so, have gathered many stories, including my first one, told to new friends and old: the story of Old Uncle Ghost, who stood praying over my feet, welcoming me to the city.

And these stories, this city, have also gathered me in.

There is a flat off Albert Street, where, if I walk past it at just the right time, I can see the echoed outlines of translucent silver hands opening the blinds, feel the warmth of a smile lingering in the air of a woman who has rented her first flat on her own for the first time. If I stay stood on that street corner long enough, I see her shape moving back and forth behind the glass. There she is, carrying bags of shopping to cook recipes she will invent herself, and years later coin as her own. There, that sound carrying on the air, just at the edge of hearing – her laugh on the phone after returning from a first date – and there, at the door, a pale wisp of a girl leaning in for a first kiss, before the wind blows and sweeps her away, leaving just peeling paint and a brass name plate bearing someone else's name, where an etching once stood that spelled her own.

I see her in the glinting white reflections of bus windows driving down Leith Walk, face half turned away, or walking down the streets now waylaid with tram works, her body moving smoothly through scaffolding and over uneven ground as if still skipping over the road that was once there. Sometimes she is frowning, as if in concentration, or other times writing in her notebook – scribbling poems that now appear in printed volumes on my bookshelves, as if they, too, hold something of her there.

There are traces of her everywhere – of her laughter, of

her sadness, of her frustration and loneliness and resilience. I think when you live in a city, and love it – choosing it for your own – a part of it plants itself in your bones, and you plant a part of yourself in it. To move through Edinburgh is to see the echoes of the selves I left behind as I moved and grew, each one a faint outline of the emotion held in that place. And as I do so, I am filled with echoes of her, different places like markers where her voice calls to my memories. It rings off tenement walls, asking to tell stories, asking to be heard. To walk through a city I have spent so long in is to walk through time: to squint through the haze of the present into the past like squinting through sleep, and there, just there – glinting off the window of the library she loved, or the wall she cried against, voice humming through the bricks like the tingle of a remembered kiss – there she is.

Perhaps this is what Old Uncle Ghost was trying to teach me, that first night before I made this city my home. That this city is filled with living echoes, and that if I stayed long enough – if I loved in it, and grew in it, and raised myself in it, transforming from the in-between girl searching for freedom on a border-crossing wind, to a writer, to a shape self-defined, solid and whole – that I may leave my own traces. That I may move through the city with the same ease of an old ghost welcoming a new visitor, running my hand along the fabric of time and find my fingers touching the hem of things lost long ago; rented flats, chalkboards, a pink kurta. And when I pull my hands back to myself, fingers solid and moving in the present moment, I will find wrapped around them a thin strand of gold.

Ten years after I met him, my Old Uncle Ghost, I returned to the walls of Rosebank Cemetery. This time my hair was covered, a light scarf wrapped around my head, as I walked through the stones. I had gone with the intention of finding him, of writing this story, and wondering if somewhere among the tall-pillared monuments, and low falling-over headstones, I might instinctively recognise his name.

I traced the walkway, the grass freshly cut and strands of it scattered wide. In the distance, on the other side of the cemetery, a man was cutting it, riding high on a lawn mower that filled the air with a faint, humming sound. I looked from grave to grave, and as I did, I met Edinburgh's different decades and centuries living side by side. There were monuments to shipbuilders and merchants and those lost too young. There were graves from before I was born and graves from after I moved to the city and graves from times in history that can no longer be accessed in living memory, but live instead in the markings of books and stone.

As I looked for Old Uncle Ghost, I met so much of the city I had not known before – stories held in memorials to its people, to those born here and those who, like me, had travelled to it and made it their chosen home. Some of the gravestones had fallen down, their markings so faded over the years that I doubt even my childhood tracing would have resurrected them. Others stood upright, defiant to time, and occasionally I'd come across small obelisks carved with cameos of those they wished to memorialise. I found even a Muslim section, with a heart-thumping echo similar to that of the one I felt on that first night. A

Khabristan, like the graveyards so familiar to me from my family memories, tucked close and neat near the entrance. Before I left, I stood by it, hands cupped – a living mirror of the visitor who had once stood over me. I whispered my own words, and hoped that they had the power to travel beyond Rosebank Cemetery – that wherever in the world Old Uncle Ghost was, they found him. That my wishes travelled over him, and that somewhere beyond that curtain I stood, voice whispering, prayers travelling across his feet.

As I sent my wishes out to him standing, hands cupped, at Rosebank's gates, I thought about how it didn't matter, not really, whether I found his name or not. I have learned that there are some things which will always be able to travel through time: feelings, favourite songs, the people we used to be, ghosts. I learned that that, truly, is what it means when we carve those words: *in loving memory*. That it is a verb, an action: memory loving, memory living, memory alive. It is acted in love, in the markings we make: in headstones, and stories, and books, and words.

In that decade since I first came to this city, since Rosebank Cemetery welcomed me with open arms – or, as it turned out, cupped hands – I had found what was calling to me, met the future that was haunting me, pulling like the whispers of freedom on the wind as I crossed the border from England into Scotland; from old into new life. As I walked past the curved stone walls marking Rosebank's entrance out into the sun, the heat of the day promising a summer like I haven't experienced in a long time, I realised that I had found the name I was looking for. That it wasn't anyone else's, living or ghost, but mine. Here in this city, I had found my name. Have made it, and everything else, my own.

In Sandy Bell's

ALEXANDER McCALL SMITH

I

OCTOBER, 1957

'Come this way,' she said, adding, almost as an afterthought, 'Matthew. You are Matthew, aren't you?'

'Yes. I'm usually called Matt. It's shorter.'

She smiled, apologetically. 'I'm terrible with names. I always have been.'

He moved towards the door. The paint was peeling off, exposing the wood below. He might offer to paint it for her perhaps. Not now, of course.

'No,' she said. 'Not down there – that leads to the drying green. We always keep the door locked.'

She gave him an appraising glance, not bothering to conceal it. He seemed a quiet young man – ideal, in her view, and she had twenty-six years of keeping students, as she put it, and her first impressions had never been wrong. He was probably feeling nervous, but that was understandable: it would be his first time away from home, she imagined, and that was never easy. Even the apparently confident ones felt it, no matter how self-possessed they seemed.

'Where you come from – Mallaig, isn't it,' she continued 'where you come from? I hear nobody ever bothers to lock. Is that true, now?'

He struggled to overcome his shyness. 'Most of the doors don't have locks anyway, Mrs Maxwell. Or if they do, the keys have been lost.' He had lost the keys to their own front door when he was twelve, and they had never been replaced. Now the lock had rusted up.

She smiled. She liked his voice. They spoke softly up there in the Highlands. One day, she thought, she might even learn a few words of Gaelic – just enough to *say* something; no, it was too late to learn anything much, and she had heard that even people who spoke Gaelic were beginning to forget it, although the old Scots words were still there – words like *dreich* and *fankle*, that were so useful because they sounded so right. But they were not talking about language, they were talking about keys and locks and Mallaig, where everybody left their doors wide open – although they would have trouble with midges, of course, and surely would have to close them on days when the midges were particularly bad – which was half the year up there. The mere thought made her brush a hand up against her face, involuntarily. She had visited a cousin in Fort William a few years ago and had been pursued into the house by a cloud of midges. Her cousin had laughed; they did not trouble her, she claimed. 'If you cover your skin with face cream, they don't like it,' she explained. 'They can't bite you through the layer.' Others spoke of bog myrtle, which you could pick yourself and that cost nothing. That was a traditional remedy against them – that, or smoke. But she suspected that nothing really worked.

'Trust,' she went on, 'that's what's lacking in the world, I think. Just my opinion. We don't trust one another because we no longer actually know who people are.' She paused, looking thoughtful. 'I remember when I was a wee girl. We lived in Tollcross and we knew everybody – on all the stairs, not just on your own. Everybody. It's different now. You can't be sure.'

They reached the door at the end of the corridor and she pushed it open. 'The boy who was in this room before you was a medical student. He's a doctor now, over in Glasgow. An awfully nice young man, he was. He was from Gourock, you see.'

He was unsure about that. Was being from Gourock a sign of respectability?

'I met his mother several times,' she continued, 'when she came over to see him. She was a widow woman, like me. Her husband had been in the merchant navy and had been killed in an accident. Something to do with a cable, I think.'

There was a man in Mallaig who had suffered an injury from a snapping cable. He had lost two fingers on his right hand. His son, Callum, was in his class at school, and had gone to work on the MacBraynes Ferries, like his father. They had walked to school together, and he thought of him now, walking back up the path to his house and turning to wave.

Mrs Maxwell was still talking about the family from Gourock. 'She was a very nice woman and she had brought her son up well. Polite. There was a daughter too, I believe. She was a great one for her swimming. She represented Scotland.'

She fixed him with a look that suggested a high bar had been set by the previous occupant.

He was not sure what to say, and so he asked, 'What was he called?'

'John Macleod,' she replied. 'John Francis Xavier Macleod. That's one name I seem to remember. The Xavier suggests . . .'

'That he was Catholic?'

She nodded. 'There are no Protestants called Xavier. None. Not that it matters to me, of course.' She looked at him again. 'I can't be doing with any of that nonsense – that sectarianism, or whatever they call it. We're all the same, aren't we? Underneath – we're all the same. Church of Scotland, RC, Chinese, Jamaican, goodness knows what – we all want the same things out of life, don't we? We need to get on, I always say. What's the alternative? More war?'

He was about to say something. He agreed: we had to get on, but he did not have the chance to say it.

'I almost got married to a Pole. He was a lovely man. Very tall. Taller than you. They're all very devout Catholics, you know. He asked me. He had been in a Polish tank regiment, and they suffered terribly, those men. Not that they complained. They just did what they had to do. Their general lived here in Edinburgh – he worked in a bar after the War. He wasn't too proud. His men saluted him when they ordered a drink.'

He looked about the room. There was a single bed, covered with a beige counterpane. There was a desk and a reading light. It was spartan, but had a polished, well-tended look to it.

She pointed to the window – one of those high Edinburgh windows, reaching all the way to the ceiling.

'If you look out there, you can just see the Pentlands. See? Over there. That's . . . oh, I forget the names of these hills. You can't remember everything.'

'No.'

She became business-like. 'The rent is payable every week, in advance,' she said. 'Two pounds, ten shillings – for which you get the room, breakfast, and dinner six nights a week. A bath is one shilling – there's an honesty box – and for heating there's that meter over there. It takes shillings, and I can always give you change if you need it.'

'Thank you.'

She nodded. 'What did you say you were studying?'

'Scottish literature.' He spoke defensively. His father had wanted him to study marine engineering. And his school principal had tried, as tactfully as he could, to point him towards law. 'You could be an advocate,' he said. 'Scott was, you know. And Stevenson. They were advocates.' And he had thought: yes, and both became writers, which is what they wanted to be in the first place.

'My, that sounds exciting. Robert Louis Stevenson?'

He smiled. 'And others.'

'I loved *Kidnapped*. That terrible uncle of his trying to kill him by making him fall off the stairs. That's the sort of thing that gives Edinburgh a bad name.'

He wanted to laugh, but controlled himself. His mother had told him that they were a very different breed down here. *Very particular*, she had said. *They don't like you to hang out your washing. Fur coats. Very small sandwiches – that sort of thing.*

'And then you'll . . .' She waved a hand in the air. 'You'll do what?'

He shrugged. 'I'll get a job, I suppose.'

She looked approving. 'You can do anything these days. Work hard, and you can do anything.'

He waited.

'There are two other students. I usually take medical students and that's what the other two are. You'll meet them. They like to go to bars.'

She looked disapproving, but only briefly. 'They have to work awful hard most of the time, poor dears. Anatomy and so on. They have to remember where everything is.' She pointed to the cupboard at the side of the room. 'John Macleod had a skeleton. They have them to learn anatomy, I believe. He kept his skeleton in that cupboard.'

He laughed. 'A skeleton in the cupboard . . .'

'That's what I thought too. Poor dead person – ending up in a medical student's cupboard.'

She left him in the room. He had his suitcase with him, and he sat down on the bed, the case open before him. His mother had packed his clothes for him and had put in a supply of the tablet that she knew he liked. She had attached a label to the small packet of confectionary and he saw that she had written, 'To remind you of home'. He picked it up and opened it, extracting a piece. It was rich and crumbly, and tasted of condensed milk. Mallaig. She might have packed a fish head, which would have been a more powerful reminder – of the harbour, the boats, the green mountainside rising sharply behind the town and the scour of Eigg across the sound. And the mewing of the gulls, and the wind; and the knowledge that all who were brought up there had instilled in them, that if they wanted to get anywhere in this life they had to go to Edinburgh or

Glasgow, even to England; that it would end, as childhood and the sense of belonging inevitably came to an end.

He unpacked. He took out his camera and placed it on the desk, carefully, almost reverentially, as one would handle a precious object It was a second-hand SLR, and was his prized possession; he had saved up for it for two long years, working part-time after school, stacking creels and fish crates, untangling ropes for the trawlermen. Photography was his hobby, his passion, and he had read that the university had a photography club and a darkroom. He would be in touch with them at the first opportunity. He picked up the camera and, pointing at the window, he looked through the viewfinder. There was a row of chimney pots and then the hills. Lowering the camera slightly, there were windows and sunlight on the window-glass. There was a woman looking out of one of the windows and for a moment he felt, guiltily, that she had seen him and was staring back. But she was waving to a friend on the street below, before closing the window and disappearing. He thought: half the time when you look at somebody they don't know you're looking at them, and their eyes are elsewhere, and that's how it is. We don't know who other people are. We don't know what we would say to them if they suddenly turned round and saw us looking.

He put the camera down. He would take photographs of this place – this strange, misty city with its closes and its passages and its eccentric, spiky skyline, all crenellations and points, and stone devices. He had four years ahead of him here. Four years of getting to know this place – four years to record it and the people who lived in it. And learn about Henryson and Dunbar and Hogg and then go back to where he came from and try to teach teenagers to read things they did not want to read. And he would get married and then discover one day that life had passed him by and that he was middle-aged and that it had been the real thing all along, and not just a practice run.

2

MAY, 1958

Ewan, one of the two medical students in the digs said to him one day, 'Jeez, Matt, you don't know you're born. I swear, you don't know you're born.' There was a note of resentment in his voice.

Matthew looked puzzled. He was wary of Ewan. 'I'm not sure what you mean.'

'I mean you have it easy – incredibly easy. You never have a lecture before ten o'clock, and then what do you do at eleven?'

He went off for coffee. He met the same friends every day: Lilian and Ted and Angus, and they went off for coffee together. But he was not going to confess that to Ewan.

'No, don't tell me. You go for coffee. Then you have lunch, right? Then maybe a tutorial – one tutorial – and then . . .'

'You think so?'

Ewan nodded. 'Yes, I do.' He sighed. 'You know what

our lives are like. Me and Iain. You know that, don't you.'

'I know you work hard. I know you sometimes have to work nights in the Infirmary. I know all that. But . . .'

'But what?'

'But I have to spend time in the library. I have to write essays.' He paused. He knew that he did not sound convincing. 'We have exams, too, you know. And we can fail them – same as you.'

They were in his room, which was smaller than the room that Ewan and Iain were obliged to share, the rent for a shared room being less than for a single. Theirs was a permanent mess, with dirty socks and shirts in a heap on the floor and an empty beer can that Iain, who smoked, used as an ashtray. Mrs Maxwell would not go into it, on health grounds, she said. 'And you boys are going to be doctors, too. Shame on you.' But she smiled indulgently, because Ewan and Iain could do no wrong in her eyes.

Now Ewan asked, 'Can you lend me a shilling. Our room's cold. It's meant to be May, but it's still cold.'

'You already owe me two. No, three.'

Ewan looked pained. 'You don't think I would forget, do you? I'll pay you back on Friday. I promise.'

Matthew opened his drawer and took out the jar in which he kept a supply of shillings.

'Your secret hoard,' said Ewan. 'You're a real miser, if you ask me. You aren't from Aberdeen, are you?'

'Very funny.'

'But that's what they're like there, believe me. They don't throw it round. Go there and see for yourself.'

He gave Ewan the coin. 'I don't want you to freeze.'

'Thank you. I take back everything I said about

you. Not that it was uncomplimentary.' Ewan paused. His face brightened. 'I met this girl today. You should see her. Unbelievable.'

'A nurse?'

Ewan looked surprised. 'How did you know?'

'An intelligent guess, I suppose.'

'She asked me out,' said Ewan. '*She* did.' He was crowing. 'She made the first move. I'm not exaggerating – I had to fight her off.'

'Are you going to bring her here?' asked Matthew. 'To your salubrious room next door? That'll impress her, I bet.'

Ewan ignored the taunt. Something had attracted his attention.

'What's that?'

'What do you think? It's a photograph.'

Ewan took the print from Matthew's desk. He scrutinised it carefully, running a finger across the glossy surface of the paper. 'You took this? With that camera of yours? You took it?'

Matthew glanced at the picture. It was one of several that he had developed the previous evening in the photography club's darkroom. He was not sure that he had given it enough time in the developer: he was thinking of redoing it. Or he might have got the exposure wrong; in which case he could try to take it again. He would see if he could get hold of the same three people – the young woman and the children she was looking after. There was something about their faces – all three of them, the woman, the young girl, the boy. There was something memorable.

Ewan was still looking at the print. 'It's very good – it really is.'

He acknowledged the compliment with a nod of his head. 'I took it on a street near the back of the Museum. Not far from the Medical School, as it happens.'

'Yes, I can see it. Just off Potterow.'

'Yes.'

Ewan pointed to the young woman. 'Are those kids hers? She looks too young. What is she? Twenty-one, two? What's her name?'

'I don't know, I'm afraid.'

He was incredulous. 'You mean, you didn't ask her?'

'We didn't speak very much. She hardly said anything.'

Ewan was watching him. 'And the kids. Do you even know what they're called?'

He defended himself. 'Not really. As I said, we didn't speak very much. She was looking after them. She helps in a shop nearby. The children belong to the woman who owns the shop.'

Ewan pointed to one of the children. 'Look at his grimy face.'

'He had been eating something sticky. It was all over his hands. He wanted to hold my camera, but I wouldn't let him.'

'Wise. Looks like treacle. You don't want a kid like that putting his fingers on the lens.' Ewan paused. 'She's nice. The girl. The big girl, I mean. Very nice.'

Matthew glanced at the photograph. It was the young woman's face that had caught his attention. There was something about it: high cheekbones, perhaps – that always helped. Or her eyes, which were hazel, and had a sort of light in them, an intelligent, sympathetic light. It was strange that eyes could do so much work – could tell you everything about what was going on within.

Matthew asked, 'Would you describe her as beautiful?'

Ewan looked at him disbelievingly. 'Where have you been? Of course I would.'

Ewan had all those girlfriends, thought Matthew. Sometimes it was a different one every week – or that was what it seemed like. Women could not resist him, but did they never see through him? He was the handsome young doctor – or would be a doctor next year. Did they never realise what he was like? He himself had only had one girlfriend so far – a girl he had met at the beginning of term, at a Freshers' dance, and he had gone out with her for three months before she had seemed to tire of him and had gone off with an engineering student who had a powerful motorbike. 'I still like you,' she said. 'We'll still be good friends – I hope.' But even as she said this, he heard the motorbike approaching and he knew it could not be.

Matthew said, 'I want to take the photograph again. I need to use a different exposure.'

Ewan gave him an enquiring look. 'You mean, go and get them together again? Get the boy to hold that bit of wood and have stuff on his face? And get her to look at the camera like that? Just like that?'

Matthew said that he would try to make it look natural. You shouldn't tell people to pose, he said; you wanted to capture them as they were naturally, doing the things they usually did. That's what gave a photograph its impact: showing people being themselves.

'So you don't ask them to say *cheese*?'

Matthew laughed. 'You don't. Who says cheese anyway – in real life? That doesn't help. People don't spend all their time smiling – its unnatural.'

Ewan had picked up the photograph again. 'When you go back,' he said, 'may I come with you?'

Matthew frowned. Why would he want to do that? They lived very different lives – Ewan and Iain had their girls and their dances at the Union and their evenings in Bennet's Bar. They led a very different life.

'I won't get in the way,' Ewan said. 'I'm just interested in seeing how you do it.'

'I point the camera and operate the shutter.'

'Oh, I know that. It's more . . . how you set the whole thing up.'

Matthew shrugged. 'If you want to. I wasn't going to do it for a few weeks yet. I've got an exam coming up.'

'Fine by me. Let me know.'

3

A FEW DAYS LATER

After his exam, Matthew went with his friends to *Sandy Bell's* on Forest Road. They sat in a corner, the four of them, and looked at one another over the rim of their beer glasses, waiting to see who would speak first about the ordeal through which they had just been put.

It was Matthew. He said, 'Oh God,' and then stopped.

Then he said, 'That's it.'

Lilian sighed. 'Me too,' she said. 'Really bad.'

They looked at Angus, who was smiling. 'No problem,' he said, and, noticing their looks of dismay, added, 'No problem – clear failure.'

The tension disappeared. 'Nothing I thought was going to come up came up,' said Ted.

'He was taunting us,' Angus joined in, *he* being the professor who had set the examination. 'That quote from . . . from who was it? I'd never heard of him. That . . . that was underhand.'

Matthew looked up at the ceiling, which was yellowed with the smoke of ages. 'There's always the resit,' he said wryly. 'We get a second chance.'

'A second chance to fail,' remarked Angus.

'We might just pass,' said Matthew. 'People do. Hardly anybody fails – completely, that is.'

Lilian was cautious. 'That's called tempting Providence. It's better to think you've failed, and then find out that you haven't. Far better.'

'You're right,' said Matthew. 'So let's stop talking about it. Subject over.'

The young men sipped at their beer. Lilian had ordered a gin and tonic. She said, 'I feel decadent, drinking this.'

'You should drink beer, like everyone else,' said Iain.

She shook her head. 'I don't like it. It makes me feel bloated.'

Matthew was about to say something, but he stopped. He touched Lilian's knee, drawing her attention to a man who had had just entered the bar.

She looked at him. 'Yes?'

'That's him,' whispered Matthew.

'Who?' asked Angus.

Matthew inclined his head in the direction of the new arrival, who was now walking towards the bar. A man on a stool rose to his feet and held out his hand for a handshake.

'That's Hamish Henderson,' said Matthew, his voice lowered. 'It's him. You know? The poet.'

Angus turned his head and stared. 'You sure?'

Matthew nodded. 'I heard he comes in here.'

'He's the one who collects the folklore,' asked Lilian. 'That one?'

'Yes,' Matthew replied. 'He goes round with his tape recorder and speaks to people who remember these things. And to singers.' He paused. 'I like his poems.'

'As much as you like MacDiarmid?' asked Iain.

Matthew hesitated. 'They're different. I like a lot of MacDiarmid, but not all. I'm not sure that I can take the whole *Drunk Man Looks at the Thistle*.'

'Or the *Hymns to Lenin*,' suggested Angus. '*Island Funeral* is more to the point.'

'And that thing he wrote about the rose . . .'

Matthew took up the quotation – how it was not the rose of all the world that broke the heart, but the little white rose of Scotland that smelled . . .

'Sharp and sweet,' said Iain.

'Yes. Sharp and sweet.'

They talked about poetry. With their second beer, and second gin-and-tonic, the examination had been forgotten. Then, at the other end of the bar, a fiddler began to play. The hubbub of conversation died and they listened.

'That's *Lochaber no More*,' whispered Matthew.

'Why is Scottish music so sad?' asked Lilian.

'It just is,' muttered Iain. 'Because this country has suffered so much.'

Angus looked doubtful. 'Has it really? More than everybody else? What about Ireland?'

Lilian asked, 'Or Greece? Or Spain? Or . . . or any of the South American countries?'

'The Spaniards,' Angus pointed out, '*caused* more suffering than they experienced, if you think about it.'

'Everybody did,' said Lilian. 'Nobody's history is perfect. Look at British history – all those colonial wars.'

The fiddler reached the end of her tune, and there was clapping, followed by a few cheers. There was laughter. Then she started again, but this time she was accompanying a singer.

'It's him,' said Matthew. 'Look.'

Hamish Henderson had been seated; now he rose to his feet. 'I want to sing a song that I wrote over twenty years ago,' he said.

Nobody spoke. Those who had continued to chat while the fiddler played sensed that this was different. They knew who this man was.

'During the war I was in Sicily,' he continued. 'I was there with the Fifty-First Highland Division. And then we went over the Straits of Messina to the mainland. When we passed through towns and villages, they came out to welcome us as liberators. The lassies ran up to the Jocks and kissed them. There were flowers.'

He sang unaccompanied. *Fare thee well ye Banks of Sicily.* Matthew thought: what could one say about this, other than *yes*. That was all. Nobody moved, and then, when he reached the end, without waiting, he began another song. 'This one is about brotherhood,' he said. 'That's all. Brotherhood.'

Somebody called out, 'Yes!'

'Aye,' said Hamish. 'Here it is.'

Matthew smiled. He knew this song, this hymn to brotherhood; he thought one day he might write about it, about how it expressed so much that was there in Scottish poetry, in Burns, and in so many others since Burns – the same message: we are brothers to one another.

And he was thinking about this when he saw her – the young woman in his photograph. He craned his neck to get a better view. She was with a small group – two other women and a man – and they were looking at Hamish Henderson as he sang. One of them reached out and put a hand on the young woman's arm. Matthew felt a sudden stab of jealousy. He did not even know her name, but he did not want her to be with anybody else. She was his discovery. He had found her with his camera lens.

After the end of the song, and of the applause that followed it, people returned to their conversations.

Lilian said, 'Just think about it. Here we are in Edinburgh, at this particular time, and we have all these poets among us. They're here. Right here.'

Angus took a sip of his beer. 'I saw Sydney Goodsir Smith. He was walking past the Kings' Theatre. In the flesh. I saw him.'

'Did you speak to him?' Iain asked.

Angus shook his head. 'What would I have said? I could hardly have—'

Iain cut him short. His tone was defensive. 'You

could have asked him about his poetry. People like to be recognised.'

'He was thinking,' said Angus. 'He was probably writing a poem – mentally.'

'Do you think,' Matthew asked, 'that people are always aware of the historical significance of their times?'

Iain made a face. 'Listen to him . . .'

'It's a serious question,' Matthew persisted. 'We look at the past and say *That was the age of whatever it was*, but do you think the people alive at the time are aware of it? Did Rembrandt get up in the morning and say, *Another day in the Golden Age of Dutch Painting*? Did Raphael think *This Renaissance is going well*, or words to that effect?'

Lilian laughed. 'Hardly. But then people would be aware that *something* was happening. They may not have had a word for it.'

'Like the Bronze Age?' suggested Iain. 'Did Bronze Age people think: *things will be better when we get to the Iron Age.*

Matthew looked up at the yellowed ceiling. *The Age of Nicotine.* 'I think they were aware of the Scottish Enlightenment – here, I mean. I think they knew that they were in the right place – here in Edinburgh – at that particular moment.'

'And the Scottish Literary Renaissance?' said Angus. 'Isn't that meant to be more or less now? Give or take a decade?'

'Perhaps,' said Matthew. And he thought: yes, this is a special moment. Something is definitely changing – coming alive after a long sleep. Edinburgh was waking up. It had taken years, and it would probably take years more, but it was happening, and they were seeing it, small signs, small glimmers. They were seeing it. And he looked about the bar to see whether he could see Hamish Henderson, find him and tell him how much he had loved reading the Cyrenaica poems, and how poetry meant so much in a world where so much was wrong. The whole edifice was rotten, but it was difficult to find just the right words to express what was wrong about it, unless you burst into song and the pain came tumbling out.

He looked about him, but Hamish Henderson seemed to have disappeared. Had he dreamt him? Had the tall figure in the curious, battered tweed hat, been somebody he merely wanted to see rather than somebody who really was there, singing in *Sandy Bell's*? And was the feeling that he felt for his friends, the love, equally illusory, like one of those light effects you saw on the water when you looked over the Sound of Sleat and the sun was just in the right position to touch the water, briefly, with mirror silver, before the blue, the green, returned?

He closed his eyes, and thought, *Why do I see things differently from other people? Or does everybody feel that – if they bother to think about it?*

Matthew rose to his feet and made his way towards the back of the bar, towards the toilets. He passed close to the young woman, and she looked up suddenly. She hesitated, obviously uncertain as to why Matthew should look familiar.

On impulse, he stopped, and smiled at her.

'You probably don't remember me,' he said.

She shook her head. 'No . . . but I think I should.' She laughed. 'Go on: tell me.'

'I took your photograph.'

Realisation dawned. 'Of course. With the kids. And Jamie had treacle all over his face.'

So the boy was Jamie. 'I thought it was something like that.'

Her companions were talking among themselves, ignoring this conversation.

'How did it turn out?' she asked.

'The photograph? Not bad. Well, actually, I got the exposure wrong. I wouldn't mind taking it again – if you don't mind.'

She would not mind, she said. And Jamie's face was permanently dirty, and so there would be no difficulty in getting him to look the same.

'I'd like it to be as close as possible to the original,' Matthew said. 'I know you shouldn't try to force things, but that's what I'd like.'

She was matter-of-fact. It was as if it were an everyday occurrence – somebody asking her, in a pub, to pose for a photograph. 'I'm there in the shop every day after three,' she said. 'I have another job in the mornings.'

'And the children?'

'After four would be best for them. Any day.'

'Tomorrow? Saturday?'

She shrugged. 'I don't see why not.'

He said, 'I don't even know your name. I'm Matthew, by the way.'

'Catriona.'

He remembered something. 'Is it all right if I bring somebody with me?'

'Why not?' she said.

He said, as an afterthought, 'And that wee boy . . .'

'Jamie?'

'Yes. His face . . .'

'Can it be dirty?' She laughed. One of the people she was with looked up, eager to share the joke. 'I told you,' she said. 'It always is.'

4

JULY, 1959

They had been worried that the day of the graduation would be rainy — the forecast had spoken of an unsettled air flow — but it was wrong and Edinburgh was bathed in sunshine. Outside the McEwan Hall the newly-minted doctors, whose graduation this was, congregated in groups with parents and friends. Ewan was there with his family and with his fiancée. He had just announced his engagement and they had managed to find a ticket for Catriona. She was wearing the ring he had bought for her from the jewellers at Greyfriars, a tiny diamond, a fragment of reflected light, barely visible, but all that he could manage. 'I'll get you something more serious later on — when I'm a consultant surgeon,' he said.

'It's perfect,' she reassured him. 'I don't want anything bigger than this.'

He introduced her to one of his classmates. 'Engaged, as of one week ago.'

'Eight days,' said Catriona, and showed the ring on her finger.

'Where are you going?' asked the friend. 'Your first house job?'

'Royal Infirmary,' said Ewan. 'Right here. Then, I hope, the Simpson. Catriona's got a job with the Council – in the Housing Department.'

Another of his friends came, and shook hands with Catriona. Somewhere nearby, one of the parents took off her hat, and it blew away. Ewan chased after it and handed it back. Catriona laughed. Ewan said, 'What can you expect with a big fancy hat? They become aerodynamic.'

Catriona looked at him, and smiled. She loved him. She had loved him, she realised, since that day he came with his friend who wanted to take her photograph. If he had not done that, then she would never have become engaged, and would not be here. *I am a doctor's wife now.* And it all came about because Matthew had seen her with those two children and had thought it would make a good photograph.

She could tell that Matthew sensed what there was between her and Ewan. She could see that he was worried about something because he had become quiet and had even been a bit impatient with young Jamie. Did he resent the fact that she and Ewan had fallen for one another? Why should he? She and Matthew were more or less complete strangers to one another – they were barely friends. He had no claim over her.

And Ewan had said to her, 'I don't want him to know about us. Do you mind? It's just something I sense. I think he might be jealous.'

She said, 'I know what you mean. But I don't think he's got any right to be jealous. He and I never went out together, or anything. All he did was take my photograph when he saw me in the street with those kids. It was the kids he wanted to get in his picture, I think.'

'Even so,' said Ewan. 'I don't want him to know.' He paused, and then confided, 'He's a bit wet behind the ears, to tell you the truth, he's from the sticks somewhere – know what I mean. Mallaig, actually.'

The woman who owned the shop in which Catriona had worked part-time also owned a small flat further down the street. The whole area lived under the threat of demolition, although it would be some years before that would eventually come about. The university was planning to demolish George Square and the streets around it for gleaming new towers. The old face of the city was being replaced with something rather different.

'You and Ewan can have the flat for a year, if you like,' she said. 'It's awfully small, but you'll be comfortable enough. And you needn't pay me any rent for the first three months – that will be my wedding present to you.'

They moved in. Ewan was busy, often being on night duty, and working long shifts. He said, 'They think junior doctors don't need sleep – they really think that. Sometimes I'm so tired I can't tell which way's up.'

'You poor thing,' said Catriona.

'I could make mistakes,' he continued.

'You won't,' she said. 'You're good at thinking on your feet, and you can do anything, as far as I'm concerned.'

She saw Matthew once, ten months after they were married. Ewan had lost touch with him after he had left the digs, and had no idea where he was living. She met him on South Bridge, going the other way, and she stopped to talk to him. He looked different: older, obviously, but also a bit more reserved. At first, she was not sure that he recognised her, but then he asked after Ewan, and she knew that he had remembered.

She decided to be direct. 'You don't hold anything against him,' she said, giving him a sideways glance. 'You weren't . . . cross that Ewan and I went out together?'

She could tell that the question embarrassed him, and she said, 'Maybe I shouldn't have asked you. I'm sorry.'

He shook his head. 'I don't care. And of course I didn't mind. It was nothing to do with me.'

She could see, though, that he *did* mind. In her experience, anybody who took the trouble to say that they didn't mind, did mind. That was not always the case, but it often was.

She changed the subject. 'Are you in the same digs?'

'Yes.'

At first, she could think of nothing else to say, but then she remembered his photography. 'Are you still taking photographs?'

He said that he was.

'That photograph you took of me and the two children . . .'

'Yes?'

'It came out all right?'

'It was very good. Maybe I shouldn't say so myself, but it was, I think. I should have given you a print. Sorry. It didn't cross my mind.'

'That wee boy,' she said. 'Jamie. He was a wee devil. He was caught stealing.'

'I'm sure he'll grow out of it. Lots of kids steal.'

'I hope so. His sister was sweet. She had a weak heart, you know. She was in the Sick Kids for months. I think she's all right now.'

'Good.'

They looked at one another. She smiled once more. He glanced at his watch.

'Of course, you have to go,' she said.

They went their separate ways. She turned round after a few yards – something made her do it – and she found that he too had turned to look over his shoulder. She hesitated, and then gave a brief wave. He returned it, and then resumed his journey.

5

MAY, 1994

'Thirty years, Matt – thirty years, more or less to the day!'

He looked down at the floor, and then shifted his gaze to the window. The school staffroom looked out to the north, to the Firth and to Fife, just visible beyond. He smiled weakly. He was not sure what to say. Was this a congratulation, or a commiseration? George, the art teacher, and the colleague to whom he felt closest, would only mean well, and so he took it as a compliment.

'Yes,' he said. 'Thirty years. And I must say I don't regret them.'

'Of course not.'

They were both silent. Was it really true that he had no regrets – he thought not. Nobody could look back on their life without at least some regrets: things you had not said to people that you should have said, and now it was too late; places you had thought you might like to have seen, but you knew you never would. You did not spend thirty years teaching in the same school, year in, year out, without thinking of at least some of the things you might have done. He remembered a poem about Walter Scott, and how his long years of writing would have cost him so much in love. He could not remember who had written that, and although he knew what the poet meant, he thought that you might say that about everything that any of us did: it cost us something in love, because you have to make a choice in committing yourself, and being in love elbowed other claims out of the way. He was sure that was the case.

This job – this job that stretched out now over three decades – had been his second teaching post. After leaving Moray House, newly registered as a teacher, he had taken a post at a school in Bathgate, and had spent the first three years of his career there. Then the Edinburgh job had come up, and he had decided to save himself the daily bus journey out to West Lothian. This new school was only streets away from the flat and the walk took him no more than ten minutes. That made a difference on winter mornings, when the buses would always be too hot or too cold and the air would be thick with the breath of humanity.

He had never married. He had been engaged once, for almost two years, and then she had been offered a job with the BBC in London. He was unwilling to live down there, in the crowds and bustle, where even the air you breathed was sixth-hand. The job meant too much to her to be missed, though, and they parted. Then he had lived for four years with a woman who eventually decided that she had had enough of sharing. 'It's nothing to do with you,' she said. 'It's just that I want my own space. Can you understand that?'

He could.

She was relieved. 'We can still be friends.'

They would not. She began to argue about who owned what, and a whole lot of suppressed recrimination came to the fore. 'You never really loved me,' she said. 'I could tell. I knew.'

He wanted to say, 'I tried' but did not. That would not have made it any better. Eventually he gave her everything, and signed a cheque to make up for almost four years' rent.

'I'm not being mercenary,' she said. 'It's just that you have your salary each month – my income is much more uncertain.'

'I understand.'

After that, he became reconciled to remaining single. He did not mind too much. The demands of the job kept him busy enough during term-time, and in the long summer holidays he would go up to Mallaig, where he still owned the small house in which his parents had lived. He had kept the house on after their death, and although it was shabby and damp, it was comfortable enough in the summer. The midges were still there, patient and unappeased, ready to pursue their programme of torment.

He continued to take photographs. He had much better equipment now, and he would often be the photographer at the weddings of friends and colleagues. His work was appreciated, and word of mouth led to more and more invitations to do this. Now, after thirty years of teaching English, he was taking the plunge and setting himself up as a wedding photographer. He would take portraits too, of course, although he knew there would be far less demand for that.

'You're lucky,' George said. 'You've got a second career lined up.'

'You could paint,' said Matt.

George sighed. 'I'd never earn anything painting.' He paused. 'No, I have to serve the full sentence.'

'I don't think you should look at it that way. How many of your pupils have gone on to the Art College? I can think of three. That's success, isn't it? You've got at least a few artistic careers going.'

'If they'd thank me for that.'

'I'm sure they would.'

'And you've done the same. You've got at least some of them to read. You've interested at least a few of them in poetry. You've got through to some of them. That counts for something.'

'Maybe. Not many, I think.'

George shook his head in disagreement. 'Even one counts for something. Even if we change only one life in our entire career, that makes it worthwhile.'

Matthew looked at him. 'Do you really believe that?'

George hesitated. 'You want me to say no, don't you?'

'Not particularly. I'd prefer to think that we've done something positive.'

George was silent. Then he said, 'You've got your exhibition, of course. That's good timing. End of your career here and the beginning of chapter two. Not bad.'

'Yes, I'm pleased about that.'

George said that he thought it could be the beginning of something. 'It could be your big moment. A real breakthrough.'

'I doubt it. It's not a big gallery, but I suppose . . .'

'You're being modest. They're highly thought-of. They get plenty of visitors, I'm told. And there was that piece about it in *The Scotsman*. That must mean something.'

He wanted to say to George that he might have an exhibition too – that it was always possible, but he realised that it was unlikely. George's painting was not very good. Somebody had described it as chocolate box school, and he was afraid that this was right. So he said nothing, and they began to talk about the small party that the Principal had arranged to mark Matthew's retirement and about how the Principal would go on for far too long in his speech, as he always did. 'He'll make thirty years seem like sixty,' said George.

'The Nero problem,' said Matthew. 'I was reading that the emperor Nero used to force people to attend concerts in which he performed. He went on forever, rather like Fidel Castro, who can speak for four or five hours, apparently. More, sometimes. Of course, you couldn't get up and walk out of Nero's performance, and so people had to pretend to die, so that they could be carried out – with a cast-iron excuse.'

'Playing dead must have been risky,' said George. 'What if you sneezed?'

'Not good,' Matthew replied.

6

AUGUST, 1995

On the fifth day of his exhibition, he dropped into the gallery on impulse. There had been an opening – a rather low-key affair, as the gallery had a limited budget for the wine that had to be served on such occasions, and there was so much else on during the Festival. He had been there, of course, and had fielded one or two enquiries about portraits. Then he had called in a couple of days later to ask how things were going, and had been told that there had been a steady stream of visitors.

'They like seeing the city as it was,' the director said. 'Those photographs you took of the Old Town – they love those. People like to remember old places. Those pictures of the Traverse Theatre when it was in the Grassmarket. People were interested in those. And that one of the tramp – the one who wore the tin helmet and had newspaper stuffed into his Wellington boots. A couple of people remembered him. Fondly.'

'He was around when we were students,' said Matthew. 'Him and another tall man who wore a Homburg hat and who used to stand at the top of Middle Meadow Walk and ask for the price of a cup of tea. We called him the Professor of Greek.'

The director laughed. 'Tramps in those days actually walked, didn't they? They never sat on the pavements.'

'They had a different story,' he said.

The director pointed to another of the photographs. 'And that one over there – that's Hamish Henderson, isn't it?'

'Yes. I wanted to take his picture for a long time and then he walked past me in George Square and I plucked up the courage to ask him. I had my camera with me, and I said 'Mr Henderson, would you mind if I took your photograph? Right here?' And he said that he would not. He said, *Bless you for asking*, and I took a few steps, because the sun was in the wrong place, as it always is, and I framed him against the building in the background, which was the office of the Scottish Dictionary.'

The director nodded. 'These people were landmarks in a way, weren't they?'

Matthew thought about this. 'I suppose every city is like that,' he said. 'There are the buildings – the places – and the people who inhabit them. The story is in both of them, I suppose.'

'Of course it is.'

'Do you think Edinburgh is still like that? I mean, do we have the same characters?'

Matthew frowned. 'It's not quite the same,' he said after a while. 'We may not have quite the same . . . how would one put it? The same civic sense – the sense of being citizens of a city.'

The director asked why this should be so.

'Because we're too preoccupied with our individual issues,' said Matthew. He was not sure how to put it, but he felt that it might be something to do with selfishness, and if there really was more selfishness, then that must be because somebody had told us that it was all right to be selfish. Moral capital did not come from nowhere. It was built up slowly, and its accumulation was hard work. And it was destroyed by selfishness – he felt sure that that was true.

'And we need to go back to what we had . . .'

Matthew hesitated. Was that the answer? To look back? Was that simple nostalgia for a past that, under close examination, was probably not quite what you thought it was? The past was never perfect – it was full of injustice and suffering, and should not be romanticised. Yet where else was there to look?

'The past reminds us—' He stopped. It was difficult not to sound trite when you had this sort of conversation. How should he finish the sentence? *The past reminds us of who we now are.* Or might one say: *of who we might be.* Perhaps that was what he really meant.

In the office at the back of the gallery a telephone rang, and the director went off to answer it. Matthew looked about him. He did not want to be found admiring his own work, and yet seeing his photographs displayed on the walls gave him a curious satisfaction.

He turned a corner, entering a small room, not much more than a large alcove, in which a dozen of his photographs from the sixties were hung. And there it was – the photograph of Catriona and the two children, the impish-faced boy, Jamie, staring out at him, and the quiet beauty of the young woman's face in the background, and the stone of the now-demolished street, and the half-light of a late afternoon, which is what he had wanted to preserve. Half-light; grey stone; north; Edinburgh; and the wind that a camera can only now and then capture by suggestion, by allusion.

He was standing in front of this photograph when the director came up behind him.

'I almost forgot,' he said. 'Somebody came in and spoke to me about that picture. A woman.'

He waited.

'That woman,' said the director, pointing at the photograph.

He drew in his breath. 'Yes?'

'She said she recognised herself in the photograph. She left a telephone number. She said that on the off-chance that you're interested in speaking to her, you might give her a call.'

He took the piece of paper that the director offered him. He tucked it into his pocket. His heart was racing within him. He felt as if he were a boy once more and that this was the mid-sixties and everything was possible.

★

7

TWO DAYS LATER

Sandy Bell's was her suggestion; he might have chosen a coffee bar somewhere, but she wanted the pub. He had forgotten so much about those days but he remembered that he had seen her there and that they had spoken briefly. He wondered about Ewan — would he be there too, but she had said *I'll meet you* and there had been no mention of him. He wondered, too, whether he would recognise her – it was more than three decades since he had last seen her, and you could not expect people to stay the same. They had been so young – now they were both in their mid-fifties. Sixty was not far off – and was there not something rather poignant about two people approaching sixty meeting in a pub largely frequented by students and young folk-musicians? He smiled. Who cared? He was reaching the age where one could say *who cares* knowing that nobody did.

Of course he knew that it was her. She was still beautiful. Her eyes still had that light in them. He saw that, and he stood up rather awkwardly. She approached him and offered her hand. It was an offer of a handshake, but it was also something else, a touching. Somewhat formally he took it. She said, 'This has been rather long.'

He said, 'Thirty years, give or take . . .'

She sat down. He offered to buy her a drink, and he went to fetch this from the bar.

Returning, he asked how Ewan was. She replied, 'I haven't heard from him for twenty-seven years.'

He was silent. He had not expected this. He felt embarrassed.

'He left me.'

'I'm sorry.'

She inclined her head slightly, acknowledging his expression of sympathy. 'Did you know what he was like?'

He hesitated. Had he known that Ewan was a womaniser? Yes.

'I suppose I knew he had a wandering eye.'

'He did.'

'And you . . .' He trailed off. He wanted to know whether she had remarried. She must have had her offers.

'I left Edinburgh. I went to work in Cambridge. I qualified as a counsellor. I worked for the university. Up until two months ago, when I came back here.' She smiled. 'It's odd, isn't it, how you can compress the story of a life into a few words like that. That's it.'

He told her about how he had retired recently after thirty years in the same school. 'I haven't done all that much,' he said. Those were the few words, he thought, that he might use to summarise his life.

'You shouldn't say that. Being a teacher is a wonderful thing.'

'Sometimes, perhaps.'

She took a sip of her drink. They were both silent. Where did one begin – after thirty years?

'Did you marry?' she asked.

He shook his head. 'Almost.'

She smiled at that. 'Sometimes it's better to almost do something than to do it.'

'That depends, I think.'

He asked whether she and Ewan had had children. She lowered her eyes and he immediately regretted his question. He started to say something, to relieve her of the need to answer, but she had started to reply.

'We had a little boy, whom we lost.'

He drew in his breath. 'I'm so sorry to hear that.'

'It was a long time ago.'

Sometimes a long time ago might seem like yesterday. 'Yes, but . . . but I'm so sorry.'

She looked at him. 'I've often thought about you, you know.'

'And I of you. I've thought about how you were here when I was with my friends.'

'And that wonderful man sang. Remember that?'

He nodded. 'I do. *Fare ye well, ye banks of Sicily . . .* Oh, those words, they make me feel . . .'

'So sad?'

'Yes.'

She said, 'Because thinking back over things does that, doesn't it?'

He said, 'There's a poem, you know, about how the onion memory makes us cry.'

'I like that,' she said.

He reached out and took her hand. She did not resist. This was how the past became the future. It made sense now. This was how it happened.

He said, 'Perhaps we could go and have something

to eat. After this.' He was not sure whether she would want that.

But she did.

Broukit Bairn

IAN RANKIN

'What brings you here?' Jim Hanson asked, hands in pockets as he exited the prison gates. A supermarket carrier bag swung from one wrist.

'I was just in the neighbourhood,' Gavin answered with a shrug.

Jim managed a thin smile. His face was almost colourless, like a piece of packaging stranded for years above the tideline of a sand-blown beach. Gavin squeezed Jim's left shoulder, feeling the boniness below the cotton jacket.

'Carry your bag?'

'I think I can manage. You got a motor?'

Gavin nodded and led the way. It was an airport rental, but he had still treated himself.

'Merc',' was all his brother said as he got in. Gavin started the engine but let it idle. 'That really annoying pinging sound won't stop till you do up your seatbelt,' he explained.

'No way to turn it off?' Jim watched as Gavin shook his head, then sighed before eventually complying. 'Time was, we were allowed to take a few risks.'

'Time was,' Gavin agreed. Then: 'Where we headed?'

'The flat. I managed to hang on to it. It's just everything else I lost. Latest tenants were told to clear out by last weekend. Better have left it in a fit state, too.'

'Or else?'

'Or else.'

They drove in silence for the first couple of minutes.

'See any changes?' Gavin eventually asked.

'I've been out a bit, you know, last couple of years. Community gardening, helping churches with their charity sales.'

'Gardening?' Gavin was stifling a smile.

'And to answer your original question, Dalry looks the same midden as when I went in. Feel free to give me the tour though.'

'Not in a hurry to get home?'

'What's waiting for me there?' Jim lowered the window and angled his face out into the air. Gavin fiddled with the console, trying to find a radio station. 'Leave it off,' Jim commanded. 'Guy I shared with, he played the worst music you've ever heard. Lyrics you couldn't make out, rattled off like machine-gun fire. Even when you could make them out they made no sense.'

'You're still a Johnny Cash man, then?'

'Best Scottish musician of all time.'

'Isn't that a myth?'

'So what? *He* believed it.'

'Where is this flat of yours, by the way?'

'You never been there?'

'You were inside for twelve years, Jim.'

'It's in Mayfield. Remember the Minto Hotel?'

'Just about.'

'Head for there and you can't go wrong.' Jim studied his brother. 'I forget, how long since you abandoned the old country?'

'Thirty years this summer.'

'Still living in London? Doing all right for yourself?'

'I get by.'

'Aye, and then some.' Jim gave a snort. 'You came north just for this?'

'I thought maybe it was a big deal.'

'Who told you? I'm guessing Sally.' Jim watched Gavin nod. 'She said to come fetch me?'

'She just thought I'd want to know.'

'I notice she didn't bother showing her face.'

'She's got a whole other life now, Jim.'

'Didn't take her long either.' He couldn't keep the bitterness out of his voice. 'Visits every week for the first two years, then she starts making excuses. I knew then and there.' His eyes were on his brother. 'Still keeps in touch with you though?'

'Not a bit of it. She tracked me down via the office, talked to my PA.'

'And you thought you'd make the trip north to remind your big brother how well you've done for yourself while he's been locked up?'

'Don't start.'

'Ach, I'm just teasing. You got a woman on the go?'

'Still a bachelor boy.'

'Mum loved that song.' Jim paused. 'Do you think Sally might see me though? Just for a drink and a catch-up?'

'Maybe give her a bit of time first.'

'Is that you speaking or her?'

'You've only been out five minutes. You might need to adjust to things.'

'What things?'

'Just stuff.' Gavin took his eyes off the road long enough to meet Jim's stare. 'Stuff generally. The world's not been sitting still, Jim.'

'Just me then.'

They drove on in silence.

After an hour, Jim had had enough, declaring the city to be all roadworks and building sites. Half the pubs he remembered seemed to have shut down or been gentrified. Most of the bookies' shops had vanished, too.

'Cafés and takeaways and charity shops,' he commented at one point, before asking to be taken home. They stopped off at a Tesco Metro for supplies, adding beer and a bottle of decent malt. The flat was a double-upper in a period property on a leafy side street.

'I think it was the place before this that I knew,' Gavin said. 'It was in a basement. Party central, as I remember.'

'Off London Road. Sally was always getting on at me for my collection of waifs and strays.' Jim brought a bunch of keys from his carrier bag. 'Don't even know what half these are for.'

'Lock-ups full of knock-off?' Gavin joked.

'You might be right. Or else the other flats I had, the ones that got sold.'

'I wasn't the only one in the family doing all right for himself.'

'You were the only one Mum was proud of though . . .'

Jim got the door open and they climbed the stairs. One more door to unlock and they were in. There was a musty smell but the place was clean enough, rubbish removed and kitchen spotless. Jim went around opening windows.

'Think they must have bought this chair,' he said, dropping into it. Gavin settled on the sofa.

'What now?' he asked.

Jim took his time studying the living room before answering.

'A pint,' he said.

The nearest place was only a three-minute walk. It had no outside tables but Jim decided it would have to do. Having bought the two drinks, he used a folded beer mat to wedge open the door. The barman didn't complain. For one thing, they were his only customers, plus Gavin had added a healthy tip when buying the round.

'That was a bit of a cheap shot about Mum,' Gavin eventually said. Jim's eyes were glued to the TV, which was showing horse racing.

'Sorry if my repartee's a bit rusty.' He glanced at his brother. 'You were always the Chosen One though. The baby, the one she doted on. I was the school-leaver, bringing in a wage so you could aim higher.'

'Little good it did me.'

'You got into uni though.'

'And dropped out again pretty damned quick.'

'Aye, that wasn't in her script. But then neither was me going off the rails. Lucky she headed north before the train crash.' He jabbed his finger ceiling-wards.

'Is Auntie Emily still around?'

'How the hell would I know?'

'Must be long dead by now. Cousins probably didn't think to tell us.'

'Wankers the lot of them. Remember playing kickabout in the back garden? Was it Joey or Jacky who tried to cripple you?'

'Both at once, I think. That's how they were.'

'And who came to the rescue?'

'You did.' Gavin raised his glass in the toast he felt his brother was expecting.

'Same as always,' Jim said.

'Apart from when you were dropping me in it.'

'Only because I knew Mum would go softer on you than if it was me. What was it she called you?'

'Her "broukit" bairn. She got it from a poem. Thought it meant cherished or something. Then we did the poem in class and it actually meant neglected.'

'The one thing you weren't.' Jim took a sip of his drink, holding the beer in his mouth before swallowing.

'Going down okay?'

'Tastes funny, but that's probably me.'

'You seem all right though.'

'How do you mean?'

'Twelve years away.'

'What were you expecting? Jail's like a long sleep, albeit one where you're on constant alert. Mind you, the first few years *I* was the one the others had to watch out for.'

'That temper of yours.'

'It was more the reputation that comes with the sentence. Go back a few decades and the judge would have been donning his black cap. Saughton's where they did the hangings, you know.'

'"Pronounced for doom".' Gavin realised he needed to explain. 'It's what the judge said if there was going to be an execution.'

'You know a lot about it.'

'I had a brother doing time. I got interested.'

'And paid lawyers a pretty penny to see if my case had any holes in it.'

'Until you stopped me.'

'You were throwing good money after bad, and handing it to a bunch of people I . . .' Jim broke off, forehead creasing in a frown. 'What's the word?' He placed the glass back on the table and squeezed both hands into fists.

'Wouldn't piss on if they were on fire?' Gavin suggested.

Jim was shaking his head. 'It's a word . . . dis-something . . . on the tip of my tongue. Ach, it's gone.'

'Disdain?'

'I don't even know what that means.'

'It means I went to university.'

'Keep rubbing it in, why don't you.' Jim pushed his glass away.

'Not going to finish it?'

'I want to go on a bus.'

'A bus?'

'Into town, aye. Then take a walk.'

'I've got the car.'

'Which is wasted in Edinburgh. Look at all the buses we were stuck behind driving here. Double-deckers, three-quarters empty. We'll be doing them a favour.'

The bus stop was just across the road. They didn't have long to wait, Jim deciding that the first one would do. He climbed to the upper deck, Gavin following. Jim's face fell when he saw that a woman had taken the front seat. He took the row behind, and when she got off at the next stop he nudged Gavin. They squeezed into the seat she had vacated.

'Nice and warm she's left it,' Jim said with a wink.

The streets opened up before them as the bus progressed. There were shops at ground level but up here they mostly had views of the windows above, the ones belonging to people's flats. There were saltires and rainbow flags in some of the windows. Others were caked with grime so that nothing at all was visible behind them.

'Used to love this,' Jim commented. 'When we were kids, I mean. Front of the bus was a treat, Mum in the seat behind checking her bag to see if she'd forgotten anything. Later on it would be just the two of us, you and me, going into town to buy records and stuff.'

'Mostly it wasn't just the two of us,' Gavin couldn't help correcting him. 'You'd usually have your gang with you. They resented me tagging along.'

'Rubbish.'

'And I'm pretty sure you resented it, too. They'd be teasing me mercilessly and you'd just stand there and watch or maybe even laugh along with them.'

'We were kids.' Jim turned towards him. 'Christ, have you been bottling that up all these years?'

'Some things are hard to pour away.'

Jim was silent for a moment before making a sound like a cackle. 'Remember that time – it was the punk phase – we were in Cockburn Street and trying to walk like the Sex Pistols and a woman across the road yelled at us to behave like human beings?' Jim began laughing.

'I don't think I was there that day.'

'You were though.'

'I've forgotten then.'

'It's an age thing. That word *will* come back to me. Just takes a bit longer for the brain to engage. Guys I was in with, half of them couldn't read or write. We had groups where they'd have other cons going through a newspaper with them, trying to get them started. I did it for a while but I just ended up getting angry with them. How hard is it to remember a handful of words?' He broke off. 'Aye, well,' he eventually said. Gavin had his phone out and was tapping the screen. 'Not boring you, am I?'

'Just checking the bus route.'

'You can do that?' Gavin angled the screen towards him for a moment. 'Well, no matter. This is us here . . .'

By which he meant North Bridge. There were plenty of pedestrians about and Jim ended up walking on the carriageway to avoid them, bicycles swerving past him. He turned into the Canongate and strode downhill, stopping outside the Museum of Childhood.

'I remember Mum bringing you here,' he said. 'I wasn't invited.'

'You had other plans most likely.'

'More than once she brought you, you loved it so much. And the Castle – pair of you had a lovely day out there, too.'

'You were never interested, Jim.'

'Maybe I would have been, with a bit of help.' Jim looked around him, taking it all in. 'I can hardly remember what I was doing a week ago, but go back far enough and it becomes crystal clear, like the water in the museum's goldfish pool – and yes, I know they've done away with that.'

'Oh – I didn't.'

'That's because you decided you belonged down south.'

'It was where I could make money.'

'Brains you've got, you could have made money right here. But then you'd still have been Jim Hanson's wee brother, no matter how rich you got.'

'I've never been ashamed of my roots. Just the opposite in fact.'

'And I'm sure it stood you in good stead. Working class, council house, single mum. I bet they lapped that up. But did I ever get a mention in your wee story? Your brother the murderer? I'm willing to bet you rubbed that bit out, like you used to do when you were checking my homework and putting it right.' Jim pointed towards the museum. 'Remember you'd come home and you'd have postcards, and coins pressed flat in one of the machines, and you'd tell me all about the mechanical toys and the ice cream you got afterwards while Mum sat with a frothy coffee. Remember?'

'Some of it,' Gavin conceded. 'But you could have been there with us if you'd wanted.'

'And break up the happy family?' Jim shook his head definitively. Gavin was about to add something, but his brother was on the move again. The way he walked reminded Gavin of those later teenage years when the city had seemed to belong to them. They toured its streets like potentates. There were traps waiting to be sprung, of course, rival gangs from other suburbs. Jim had learned how to fight, while Gavin had become fleet of foot and good at hiding, finding nooks and crannies down all the closes and wynds, much like the one they were descending now with the Cowgate waiting below.

'Haven't had this much exercise in a while,' Jim was saying. 'I used the gym, first few years, but then I got

bored of it. Still kept in shape though – stopped the . . .
coming for me. In any nick, it's survival of the fittest.'

'Stopped the what coming for you? Predators?'

'That's it, aye. Predators. Had to give a few of them a
doing. Thing to learn was not getting caught, otherwise
the screws had to dole out punishment. Bit of solitary or
whatever. Messes with your head.'

'You did get caught then?'

'Once or twice.'

'I heard you thumped one of the guards, too.'

'Learned not to do that again. Ten against one when
they came for me. A week in the hospital after.'

'Were you okay, though?'

'No worse than before. Don't remember this street
being so steep.' Jim stopped for a moment, looking both
ways. 'You'd be all right running down it, but up would
be another matter entirely.'

'Didn't stop you chasing those Liberton boys up it one
time. Three of them and one of you.'

'And still they ran.'

'You were pretty well known by then.'

'I suppose I was.' Jim looked at his brother. 'What did
Sally tell you?'

'How do you mean?'

'To bring you scampering north.'

'Just that you were getting out. She thought you might
appreciate a friendly face.'

'Right enough. Not much of a parade waiting for me
otherwise. Need to track down some of those old faces,
ask them why they never came to see me, or else stopped
after the first few visits. I know a fair few couldn't risk it

– you get tested for drugs before you're allowed in – but I like to think I knew a few non-junkies back in the day—'

He broke off. 'Anyway, it's good to see you, and I know pretty soon you're going to try to shove some money my way. I'll probably take it, too. Not because I need it but because it'll make it easier for you to leave. Conscience salved and all that. You'll have felt you've done what you can for your poor lost soul of a brother.'

'Christ, Jim . . .'

'Tell me I'm wrong.'

Gavin stretched out his arms. 'Of course I'd want to help you get back on your feet.'

'Then invite me to London, give me a job in your firm. I can kip on your couch till I get a place of my own.' Jim's mouth widened in a smile. 'The look on your face.'

'No, it's just . . .'

'I don't want any of that, Gavin. London's your dream, not mine.' He squeezed his brother's forearm and began walking again, turning right along the Cowgate's narrow pavement. Gavin remembered something from a school or university lesson: Robert Louis Stevenson's description of Edinburgh as a 'precipitous city'. Yes, you could climb Arthur's Seat or Calton Hill or look down on to the New Town from the heights of the Castle ramparts, but you could also be at the bottom of a chasm like the Cowgate, with the city almost impossibly out of reach above. Walking beneath South Bridge could feel like being an insect deep underground, invisible to the majority, easy to forget about. Jim was right, too – Gavin had always been their mother's favourite. How big a part had that played in Jim's development? He had grown away from them, spending more time roaming the streets, skipping school, hanging around shops and recreation grounds. Taking drugs eventually, and dealing them soon after, realising that his mixture of guile and brawn could make him money, leading to a further estrangement from family and home.

It was a question often posed: were people born bad or made bad by circumstance? Not that Gavin thought of Jim as bad. He'd met worse; he'd certainly met people more venal and ruthless. Jim had done a terrible thing but that didn't in itself make him bad. Gavin thought back to those games they'd played – cowboys and Indians; opposing armies. The comics they had read had been full of goodies and baddies, no blurring, no grey areas. Heroes and villains, easy to tell which was meant to be which.

Jim had come to a stop outside an anonymous piece of frontage. Gloss black paint. A padlocked door. No windows. A sign above advertising a brand of imported beer. Gavin realised that this had been their destination all along.

'It's not called the Brandy Snap any more,' Jim said.

'I'd imagine precious few nightspots have the names they had when you used to haunt them.'

Jim was staring down the Cowgate's roadway. 'I should have let him get away,' he said.

Gavin had been four hundred miles away in London, had heard about it only the next day when Sally phoned him in tears. He knew the details now, of course, knew them to the minutest degree, thanks to the money he had paid to have lawyers and even a private detective look into the case. A man had insulted Sally as she walked back to her table from the toilets. Well, that's what someone whispered in Jim's ear at any rate. Sally always said that she couldn't remember. The music had been loud and she hadn't really been listening. Maybe the person who told Jim had done so because they wanted something to happen.

And something certainly happened.

A confrontation. A denial followed by a drunken shove. The victim making his way out of the club, Jim following. Jim reaching him, hitting him, kicking him to the ground and those kicks continuing, pounding the man's head against the edge of the kerb. A murder charge. The defence had argued in court for culpable homicide . . . mitigating circumstances . . . a drunken outburst completely out of character. Sally had testified to the insult, though in private she confided that she didn't really know. Jim, of course, was not unknown to the police. They had tried several times to put him away for dealing drugs. The defence had used this as part of their argument, too. A local businessman and protective boyfriend, harried by a vindictive police force.

Verdict on day three: guilty.

Barlinnie, and then Peterhead, and then Saughton. Three different prisons in twelve years. They had taken their toll. The spark behind Jim's eyes was fainter, the body frailer and more hunched. A man of sixty who could have passed for a decade older.

'Should have let him get away,' Jim repeated quietly. 'But my blood was up. I had a name, remember, a legend that had to be protected.' He paused. 'What's the other thing called? The thing that isn't a legend?'

'A myth?'

'That's it. Never really known the difference. I'll bet you do though.' He watched Gavin nod. 'Knew you would. My brainy broukit bairn of a brother. Wonder how different it would have turned out.'

'If you hadn't gone after him, you mean?'

Jim nodded. 'Two lives stopped at that moment. I mean, he was a wanker, everyone knew that, but even so. The only thing I really remember is the car. It was coming towards us and its lights were on. I saw the blood on my shoes and I stopped and turned. Must be what it's like to be an actor on stage. They only pulled up for a second though, then they drove past, and I left him there and went back to finish my drink. Bouncers tried to stop me going in. I reckon it was one of them that phoned the filth.

'It was.'

Jim nodded again. 'When I was led out, I saw my own bloody footprints facing the other way. 'One of youse will need to wash that', I told them. He paused, releasing a lungful of air. 'You don't smoke, do you?'

'No.'

'I gave up last year. Wouldn't say no to one right now, though.' He took a step towards his brother. 'She did say something though, didn't she? Sally, I mean. Know how I know?'

'How?'

'It's because you've not asked why I was let out early. Makes me think you don't need telling. Compassionate grounds is the term. See? Some things I can remember straight off. Me and Megrahi – both of us released on compassionate grounds. Maybe I'll even live as long as him. Doubtful though.'

'Alzheimer's can be slowed right down, Jim. The rate of cognitive deterioration, I mean. I've been reading up on it.'

'I'd be disappointed if you hadn't. Story of your life, Gavin. Hungry for knowledge. Sally doesn't know the whole story though.'

'How do you mean?'

'Alzheimer's is only half of it. There's a tumour, too. Fair-sized and not going anywhere. Unlike us. We're going to the Grassmarket so you can buy me a whisky. Then we'll take the bus back to mine and break open that bottle, maybe hit a chip shop on the way if any still exist. That wee phone of yours will doubtless tell us. You'll want to be heading back tomorrow, but we can make a night of it. If the sofa's not enough, you can always find a hotel. Actually, we didn't check for sheets and stuff, did we? I've no idea if there's any of that in the flat. I only saw a hand-towel in the bathroom. You okay, kid?'

You okay, kid?

Suddenly Gavin was twelve again, doing his big brother's homework for him, traipsing a few steps behind him and his friends, waiting outside the shops while they went in to lift stuff. Jim would never let him take part – *Mum would leather me.* Then there was his first taste of alcohol, Jim's hand rubbing his back as he threw up, and the first time he asked a girl out and she turned him down with a snort of laughter. Jim had found him curled beneath his single bed, and had crawled right in there with him.

You okay, kid?

And much much later, at their mother's funeral, well-enough attended by neighbours and family, as the curtain closed on the coffin and the music played, hinting that it was time to leave the crematorium so it could be readied for the next on the conveyor-belt, everyone waiting for them to lead the way up the central aisle of the chapel to the door, Gavin's eyes blurry with tears, and Jim's arm reaching across his shoulders.

You okay, kid?

'I'll be fine,' he managed to blurt out.

'Of course you will. I want to hear all about this high-roller life of yours. Anything to take my mind off where I've just been. You can even lie if you want. Penthouse orgies, private jets full of champagne, Grand Prix parties in Monaco . . . I'll believe anything you tell me.'

'I've become a pretty convincing liar down the years.'

'I don't doubt it.'

'But truthfully, I don't need to head straight back to London. The business more or less takes care of itself these days. I'm just a figurehead who's left twiddling his thumbs.'

'So I'd be doing you a favour by keeping you here?'

'For as long as you need me.'

'Straight to the airport then after these next whiskies.' Jim laughed and put his arm around his brother. 'Only joking. It's nice of you to offer.'

They had strayed off the narrow pavement. A car sounded its horn as it neared them from behind. When Jim kept hold of Gavin, ensuring the two of them stuck to the road, the car slowed only a little before manoeuvring past them and roaring into the distance. Gavin watched it fade from view.

As soon as Jim would let him, he stepped up on to the relative safety of the pavement, hauling his brother after him.

On Portobello Prom

SARA SHERIDAN

It's rainy days in the middle of the week that I like best: sitting in a booth at Ferrari's with a banana split. In the mirror we look like two girls in an American glossy magazine. Mrs Ferrari had the place done up last year with loads of chrome and tiles and red leather. She wanted to change the name to Ferrari's Milk Bar but Mr Ferrari wouldn't have it. 'Ferrari's is enough,' he pronounced. And what Victor Ferrari says tends to go.

Today it's only Violetta and I in the place – our hair held back with brightly coloured bands and so much mascara we could swat flies with our lashes. Violetta puts down the sundae on the table and slips into the seat opposite me. Your average banana split is just banana with ice cream, whipped cream and chocolate sauce, but for us, Violetta adds a scatter of cherries and a layer of caramel and calls it a 'Caribbean Royale'.

'Imagine if you could get vanilla ice cream but with caramel already in it,' I say meditatively.

'Then we wouldn't be able to sell the sauce separately,' Violetta points out as if I'm a dummy.

I love it at Ferrari's. I've been coming on rainy weekdays since we left school and Violetta started to work full time for her parents. I was plucking chickens at Aitken's but then I met Duncan at the Plaza and he offered me a room in his house on Marlborough Street and ten shillings a week, taking snaps of day-trippers on the Prom. I'm his best click-click girl. I have a way with the punters. I think that's because I like them – the whole lot from wee boys with stripy shirts and rubber armbands to old ladies in flowery cotton summer dresses, floppy straw hats and black, winter handbags slung over their forearms. 'Give me a smile,' I say and ham it up with a wink like I'm David Bailey. And they smile all right and later they buy the picture. I take snaps at the Plaza now too: Thursday, Friday and Saturday nights. Duncan came to an arrangement. The photos aren't as much fun. Everyone dresses up the same to go dancing when it comes down to it, which is different from the beach where people get to be themselves. Still, I like the music and the lads on the door are decent, always joking around.

Today as the rain tips down into the rolling, slate grey sea, Violetta is downhearted. I say today, but Violetta has been downhearted pretty much since she started at Ferrari's. I don't get it myself. I'd say, in the scheme of things, Violetta has it easy. Working at Ferrari's has to be a dream – inside in the warm and nothing but happy punters. Who doesn't like ice cream? Nobody. Though business-wise it's got to be tough taking on Arcari's because they have the best pitch for ice cream in the whole of Portobello. This is a problem that Duncan does not suffer from. No other bastard would dare take photographs along the Prom. But the Italians do it differently. Not in Glasgow as I understand it. But here, sure, they make out like they all get along and nobody's turned up dead yet in the open-air pool overnight, taking a midnight swim.

'What do you think?' Violetta asks, smoothing the vanilla over the banana with her long spoon.

'You did something different?' I'm wary, because this is of the utmost importance to my pal. Honestly, one vanilla tastes much the same as another. Everything Violetta makes is delicious. But for her, it's life and death. She says it's bad enough only being allowed to make three flavours. She might as well make them the best.

'I put in some cinnamon,' she whispers confidentially. 'It brings out the vanilla.'

My mouth is so cold that I can't taste anything any more, and I'm only still eating because the texture is like frozen satin melting on my tongue, but I make a noise as if this is huge news. Headlines all round. 'Delicious,' I say.

'I think it makes it,' Violetta says and promptly bursts into tears.

This is not the shock you might expect. Violetta is a chick who cries a lot. But I get out of the seat on my side of the table and slip in alongside her. I put my arm round her shoulder. 'Hey hey,' I say and make comforting noises. 'What's wrong?'

Violetta peers out of the booth dramatically, as if checking nobody can overhear, but Mama and Papa Ferrari don't work on rainy days. There's nobody in the place but Violetta and me. The last customer left half an hour ago after sitting over a scalded milk for ages, hoping the weather would change. She strains to look through the window onto the Prom, where a woman is struggling to keep a grip on a shopping basket and an outsize golfing umbrella at the same time. The wind's started up. Once the wind gets going you can quit for the day. A shower or two and people will thole it if there's sunshine, but it takes a particular kind of person to persist through cloud, showers and a howling gale. Once or twice I've seen a family set up a windbreak with a brolly over the top. Then they send their kids down to paddle in the water in wellington boots and bathies. But those people never want their photographs taken. I can't say it's an experience I'd want to remember either.

'I'm getting married,' Violetta sniffs.

This is not what I was expecting. The woes of Papa Ferrari refusing to allow her to sell orange sorbet or Mama Ferrari policing Violetta's skirt length – yes. But this sounded like real trouble.

'Married? To whom?' I ask.

Violetta pulls a crumpled handkerchief from her sleeve. 'Giorgio Fabrizi. He's my second cousin,' she sniffs and blows her nose.

To me this sounds dodgy. Not dodgy like Duncan's arrangement with the McGuigans for his share of the Arcade money, but still.

'You can't marry your second cousin,' I say like I'm an advocate dismissing a case with a guffaw over port and cigars.

'You can,' Violetta insists, earnestly. 'I should be happy about it. The Fabrizis are gelato royalty. They've been in the game for more than a century. They started out with a stall, selling penny licks in Milan,' she adds, touching the handkerchief lightly to her eye as if that is going to fix her eyeliner, which it is not. She gets up and sighs at her reflection in the big mirror on the other side of the café, smoothing her hair and peering in disbelief at the uneven, dark rings that have appeared under her eyes. She's going to have to start again with the make-up. 'Here,' I say, taking my hankie from my handbag and licking it. You can't remove eyeliner dry.

It takes longer to patch her up than it did to ruin the make-up in the first place but I get out my Rimmel and set to, while Violetta continues to divest herself of her troubles and fiddle with the yellow headband holding back her long, dark hair.

'We need to expand, and Uncle Fabrizi is prepared to invest, but he wants someone from his side of things on the spot.'

'Couldn't he just send your cousin to work here?'

This, Violetta assures me, is not the Italian way.

'Well, is Georgio nice?' I ask.

Violetta nods but I can see she is close to ruining all my good work again. She bites her lip and I'm happy to say this holds back the tears. 'I can tell you, Rosie, can't I?' she says.

'Of course you can,' I assure her. I'm taken back she even has to ask, because as far as I'm aware Violetta has never kept a secret from me, not since we first met in Miss Mitchell's class when we were seven and got rid of our free milk down the drain at the back of the janitor's shed at break.

'I'm in love,' she whispers.

'In love?' I repeat. I can't even imagine. I'm not the type to go mooning about – I've seen too much in my nineteen years. Lads bringing different girls to the Plaza week on week. I know what goes on down the lane – sometimes, during summer, it isn't even dark yet. It's not that I've never fancied anyone. Sure I have. I've necked on the sand after midnight with the best of them. But love? That's an entirely different matter.

'It's Henry,' admits Violetta, guiltily.

'Henry Campbell?' I say, trying not to shriek. 'But he's so—' I manage to stop myself in time. Henry Campbell was at school with us. He's a skinny wee guy who won the maths prize. Every year. He has nice brown eyes, right enough but honestly, I can't picture him with Violetta; not for the life of me. When Violetta decides to keep a secret it turns out it's going to be a big one.

'We've been seeing each other for a while,' she admits.

I'm about to ask a question when two half-drenched kiddies bundle through the door, counting their pocket money and staring at the sign over the freezer to figure out what they can afford. Violetta returns behind the counter.

'What flavours have you got?' one of the kids asks.

Violetta sighs. 'Same as always, Malcolm.'

The kid waits stubbornly. As far as he's concerned Violetta reciting the flavours is an important part of the experience and one that he is not about to forgo. After a few seconds Violetta gives in. 'Vanilla, chocolate or strawberry.' It galls her to say it. If it was up to Violetta there'd be Rose and Pear and Lemon. There'd be Rum and Raisin. And Orange Sorbet. And a whole counter of homemade marshmallows and fruit jellies. Violetta has always ploughed her own furrow. She made snowballs without coconut last year when her parents went down to North Berwick to see an old friend for the day. Sales of the coconut-less snowballs almost doubled that weekend, which I think is because Violetta put up a sign that called them Nude Snowballs. Mr Ferrari was furious. He's a traditionalist down to his black leather shoes, replete with a high shine and slicked back hair that he will never admit to dying. 'Snowballs without coconut aren't snowballs at all,' he muttered furiously and I have to say, he had a point though Violetta's trial run clearly establishes that most right-thinking people think snowballs are better without.

The kid considers his options. 'Strawberry,' he says decisively and lays sixpence on the counter. Violetta snaps her metal scoop in and out of the water.

'Just the one. Double scoop?' It's the right money.

The kid nods. 'We're sharing,' he says.

Smart kid – buying in bulk.

Violetta serves this ice cream like she serves every ice cream – even on the busy days. As if it's a work of art. Today she's feeling generous. Swathes of creamy strawberry pile up on the cone. It's more than a double scoop, it's a hand-held gelato sculpture. The kids can hardly believe it as she hands it to them and the pair of them rush outside and disappear along the sand as if they've got away with robbing a bank. Violetta shrugs. I guess she thinks somebody might as well have a great day.

And that's when I see him cutting along the Prom. He's wearing a navy suit with a dapper-looking raincoat over the top and a thin, red scarf. Violetta smooths down her pink, nylon apron and I realise that this absolute dish coming towards us is Giorgio. It has to be. He opens the door and breezes in.

'Vi!' he says with a smile like sunshine.

And then I realise that there's something wrong. Not wrong with Giorgio, if you get me. He's perfect. Straight out of the *Gentleman's Quarterly* or maybe *Esquire* magazine. But there's something wrong between them.

Giorgio hangs up his raincoat on the chrome coat stand and I get a few more seconds to figure it out. Then I get it. He reminds me of the lads in the Men's Sea Swimming Club. Fair play to them. Once a month, rain or shine or even, on one occasion, snow, the Men's Sea Swimming Club meets at the far end, past the pool. The first few times it put Duncan in a rage, I can tell you, but those guys wanted their photographs taken. We sold every shot, which took the edge off Duncan's moral outrage. Because the Men's Sea Swimming Club are homosexuals – every one of them. Just a bunch of guys getting undressed together in public because getting undressed in private might land them in court.

'If that's your thing though, where are you supposed to go to meet?' I said to Barbra who works in the change booth in the Arcade. Barbra looked over the top of her new spectacles, which are the shape of cats' eyes, and of which she is extremely proud. 'In Saughton?' she said drily. And then, after consideration added, 'But what do they do? It can't be natural.'

But working on the Prom the last year has divested me of any ideas I ever had about what's natural and what isn't. I get to meet all sorts. Odds and sods, Duncan calls them. But he's happy enough to print postcards when I snap the odds and sods because it's those people who capture summertime at the beach best of all: a bearded lady sunning herself on a deckchair, a kid with a hare lip eating one of Violetta's huge ice creams or a skinny old man perched precariously on Jock the donkey. The

Kodak rep looked at the postcards for a long time when we started selling them. 'Are these folk all right with this?' he asked. It hadn't occurred to me, or to Duncan to ask for permission. Duncan, after all, has been doing whatever he wants for years with no opposition from anyone and me, well, I just figure if the pictures are good, people will be fine about them. 'The postcard range has proved very popular,' Duncan said steadily and the Kodak guy didn't press his point. Come to think of it, the most popular postcard we have is a picture of three blokes from the Men's Sea Swimming Club, with their arms around each other, fresh out of the water, smiling like lunatics. It's right there for anyone who cares to look and I can't say it doesn't surprise me that the polis have never copped on. Maybe they don't want to. Better the Men's Sea Swimming Club, is out in the open perhaps.

Giorgio holds out his hand as Violetta introduces us. He's wearing a natty gold watch with a patent, crocodile strap. The end of his nails are pale and shaped like the moon when it's only a sliver. There's something glossy about him. He's wearing aftershave that smells like cedarwood. I bet he's twenty-one.

'Nice to meet you, Rosie,' he says.

Then he disappears behind the counter to make a cappuccino. He just helps himself. I search Violetta's face to see if she's realised. Maybe that's why she's reticent. Henry Campbell indeed. But there's no inkling, just like the polis. Giorgio clears the remains of our Caribbean Royale and then sits down and adds sugar to his coffee from the shaker, stirring thoughtfully.

'So, were you two at school together?' he asks.

I nod.

'And what do you do now, Rosie?'

I tell him about being a click-click girl. I mention that I work for Duncan but the name sparks no recognition in Giorgio's eyes. Oftentimes guys sit up a bit straighter when I tell them who I work for.

'So, when's the big day?' I ask.

Giorgio stirs his half-drunk cappuccino some more. 'We've got a lot to sort out before that,' he says, which, let's face it, at the least, lacks romance. Poor Violetta, I think, but Giorgio continues oblivious, 'I thought I'd head down to Musselburgh to look at some premises,' he adds. 'You could close the shop and come along – if you'd like, Vi.'

'Close the shop?' Violetta echoes.

'Yeah,' he says. 'It's bowfing out there. Nobody's going to want ice cream on a day like this.'

I'm not Italian but I know what Papa Ferrari would think of this proposition and it would not be positive. There can be thunder tipping out of the clouds and so much water running down Bath Street that there's a puddle on the Prom the size of the kiddies' pool, but Ferrari's is always open. However, Violetta takes off her pink, nylon apron and hangs it behind the counter, slipping on the yellow coat she got from C&A last year and picking up a brolly from the stand. She pulls the shop key out of her pocket.

'All right,' she says. 'Let's go.'

Outside, Violetta locks up. I'm about to say goodbye to them and head back to the photo booth when who should peel around the corner but Henry Campbell. I don't know what Mrs Campbell has been feeding her son of late but he's grown since the last time I saw him, which was at the leavers' prize giving ceremony at school four years ago. Firstly, he's bigger – taller, I mean. And secondly he's almost as nicely dressed as Giorgio, in a chocolate brown suit with tapered trousers and a parka over the top. His hair is to his collar, like those Beat guys in the clubs up Leith Walk. Violetta lets out a wee sound like a puppy having a bad dream.

'Letta,' says Henry, with some urgency. 'Is it true?' He eyes Giorgio. 'Who are you?' he asks.

Giorgio looks for a moment as if he isn't minded to reply. 'Giorgio Fabrizi,' he says eventually and when he smiles you'd swear the sun had come out again though his eyes are hard this time.

Violetta stumbles over what she has to say. 'Giorgio is my second cousin,' she manages.

'This is the guy you're marrying?'

I don't blame Henry for not believing it. I can hardly believe it myself. For other reasons. Still.

'What about me?' Henry says. 'What about us?' he adds.

Giorgio glares at Violetta. 'Vi,' he snaps like she's a dog who has been naughty. 'Who is this person?'

Violetta looks at me and I know that I'm going to have to say something.

'Henry was at school with us. He's an old friend,' I cut in.

'Hi Rosie,' Henry says as if he's just noticed me. Maybe he has. I can't help thinking this would make a great photograph – two well-dressed guys squaring up to each other with white-grey storm clouds overhead. The light is perfect – cold and flat. The composition has drama.

'Vi is my fiancée,' Giorgio puts his arm around Violetta's shoulder and she freezes – not in a soft way like good ice cream but like a lemon ice-lolly on a stick. And not a happy lolly. The kind your auntie chooses when she wants to lose weight.

'Did you buy her a ring?' Henry asks Giorgio as if he's throwing down a glove like an 18th century nobleman. He reaches into his pocket and brings out a wee green box. He opens it. Inside is a sweet diamond ring in the shape of a flower – a daisy I think. It's the kind of thing Violetta loves. Her eyes widen. 'I bought you a ring. I'm serious about you. About us. Will you marry me, Letta?'

This photograph has changed exponentially, I think. Now it's a Valentine's Day card of sorts. But it doesn't last long. Giorgio lets go Violetta's shoulder. He squares up and punches Henry. The box falls from Henry's hand and skitters over the edge of the paving onto the sand as he reels. Giorgio hits him again. There's a lot of misconceptions about queers being soft, but the Men's Sea Swimming Club are hard bastards who'll swim in the Firth in January as well as in June and they can fight, all right. They're used to having to.

Along at the arcade Big Rob McGuigan appears in the doorway as if an alarm has sounded to herald a fist fight on the Prom. But Violetta steps in.

'This isn't Italy, Giorgio,' she snaps.

Giorgio can't argue with this. He only has to look round to establish it is not. 'No brawling,' she says in a tone of great authority.

She huckles her fiancé back to her side and Giorgio controls his temper.

'Come on,' Violetta insists. She glances at me and her eyes say, 'Take care of it, will you?' And then clamped onto Giorgio's arm she guides him up Regent Street and disappears round the corner. The Ferraris always park on the lane.

I nod in Big Rob's direction to say I've got this one and he disappears back inside the arcade. Henry gets to his feet and stares after Violetta. He looks like he's going to cry.

'Poets are damned but they see with the eyes of angels,' he says.

'What?'

'It's Ginsburg.'

I regard Henry. He's changed a lot since school but once a swot, always a swot, no matter how cool he looks. 'You're serious about Violetta then,' I say. It isn't a question.

Henry nods. 'I've found us a place in town. Those old Georgian buildings are lovely and nobody wants to live in the New Town any more. It's a long game – it's all about term. But those houses are built properly. I think it'll be a good investment.'

I raise my eyebrows. 'A good investment?' I repeat. And that is a question.

'I've almost saved enough to buy a place,' he adds.

'*Buy* somewhere?'

Henry nods and goes over to retrieve his engagement ring from the beach.

'It's lovely,' I say. 'It's just her kind of thing.'

Henry's brown eyes warm to me. 'He's not going to make her happy,' he says. 'He doesn't get her at all.'

I have to agree. 'I think it's a family thing,' I add.

Henry suggests going up to Di Marco's Café but I sense if we're going to discuss Violetta and Giorgio we ought to go somewhere a lot less Italian, so instead I say let's go to the Cullen. We settle in the corner and Henry buys me a bitter lemon and gets himself a half of stout to aid his recovery from the fight. Turns out he's been making money playing cards. 'Poker mostly,' he says, lighting a Capstan and puffing like a pro. 'High stakes.'

It turns out Maths isn't boring once you apply it. He also races cars at the weekend, which he confides has a lot do with geometry. I think back to our last year at school. Half of our crowd are married now, mostly settled and renting near their parents. Nobody I know has moved into town and bought a place.

'So, you're in love,' I say, taking him more seriously now.

Henry gives me a look that says, I bought a ring, of course I am. 'I could use some help,' he replies.

I finish the bitter lemon. 'I'll see what I can do,' I promise. But I'm not sure what I can do. Violetta, after all, has to make up her own mind.

Thursday night at the Plaza is always quiet and tonight it's even quieter than usual on account of the weather. There isn't even a queue. Tommy, the bouncer, shelters in the doorway out of the rain and inside, I sit at a table drinking Vimto. The Plaza doesn't sell Vimto but Dickie, the barman, keeps some behind the counter as if it's contraband. Just for the staff. I'm tapping my feet. They've decided to play belters tonight – the Shirelles and Barry Mann and later Patsy Cline, but there aren't many decent snaps to be taken on the dance floor. It's young love that sells and zero young lovers have come out tonight, in the rain. I take a sly shot of three teddy boys drinking half pints of shandy at the bar. The light from the glitter ball catches their Brylcreemed hair and I have to say, those crêpe-soled shoes are cool. A couple of years ago I'd have laughed at them, but I suppose you get used to things. Up the back two Beat types are staring dead-eyed at the sparse crowd while they knock back Camparis. I don't know why they came in – maybe it's not a good night to head west. It was beating down rain earlier and it'll pelt down again soon.

I'm on the point of leaving early to head back to my bedsit because there's no point in flogging a dead Thursday night, when I see Giorgio on the other side of the road, getting out of a cab. I wave from the doorstep of the Plaza and bid Tommy goodnight. Halfway across the street I can see Giorgio is in a temper again.

'What's happening?' I ask, casually, stepping onto the pavement next to him.

As he focuses on me, Giorgio's eyes are blazing like beacons in the glossy black night. 'It's that guy,' he says. 'How could she?'

I pull my ciggies out and offer him the pack. We both take one. Giorgio lights me and then himself. 'She should have told me before,' he says. 'If Vi doesn't want to marry me, that's her decision. He pauses and takes a deep draw. 'I don't think Yolanda will ever get over it.'

Yolanda is Violetta's mother – Mrs Ferrari to me. If

Violetta is prone to bursting into tears, Yolanda takes it up a notch. When the Skylark broke free of its moorings a couple of years ago and smashed into the Prom, she got practically operatic.

'Yolanda's upset is she?'

Giorgio nods. 'I was there tonight. Vi only went and got engaged to that . . . that . . .' he sounds like he's going to explode.

'Henry,' I cut in. 'His name is Henry.'

'Well, Henry turned up during dinner.'

I let the seriousness of this sink in. Dinner at the Ferrari house is sacred.

'Violetta has some timing,' Giorgio spits. 'He rang the doorbell and they asked him to join us – well, they didn't know did they? And then Vi just kind of announced that he'd proposed and she'd accepted his offer and it was off between us. She said she wanted to tell everyone when we were all together because I'm family too.' Here he raises his eyebrows in punctuation. 'Yolanda was bringing the chicken cacciatore out of the oven but she lost her grip,' he adds. 'The casserole shattered all over the floor.'

This sounds extremely serious. All the years I've been hanging around with Violetta, Mrs Ferrari has only ever made us spaghetti for dinner and she's never dropped it once. Also, I happen to know that Yolanda Ferrari inherited her grandmother's pots and pans, not from the old country – only from Newington. Still, shattering any old casserole would be one thing, but Nonna's pots are both irreplaceable and sacred.

'God,' I say and grind out my ciggy with the sole of my shoe. 'I'm sorry.'

A bus swishes past through a puddle that has formed at the kerb. We both step back instinctively, almost like we're dancing.

'The buses look different in Glasgow,' Giorgio says as if he's feeling nostalgic for the West Coast. 'It's the livery, I suppose. You went with friends?' He nods towards the Plaza.

'I work there,' I say.

He raises his hands to his face as if he's holding a camera. 'Click-click?'

'Not so much click-click tonight,' I admit. 'Hardly anyone in the place.'

'You make people look good,' Giorgio adds. 'You took those postcards, didn't you? You have a great eye. I think they'd look good as bigger prints, you know. Framed. On the wall.'

I can feel myself blush. Just the way he says it, with some kind of respect in his voice, as if I'm an artist. Nobody ever talks about my snaps like that. He walks me round the corner to my gate. Most of the lights are off in the house – everyone has gone to bed early. It's that kind of day. The night air feels like silk on my skin. 'Maybe it's for the best,' I say, turning to go inside. 'I think Violetta will be happy with Henry.' These are not words I ever thought would come out of my mouth but it's obviously a love match.

Giorgio stares in the direction of the strip of sea at the bottom of the street, which today is so dark, the blue is almost black against the wide night sky and it's difficult to tell exactly where the water and air meet. 'Happy,' he says as if this notion is beyond him.

'You can still work with the Ferraris, you know. Expand the business, I mean.'

Giorgio shrugs. 'I suppose,' he says.

We stand there like idiots. One of the streetlamps is on the blink and it goes on and off every now and then, changing the shadows. 'Well, goodnight,' I say.

I turn to go inside. The gate creaks and tonight it sounds sad somehow. In my room I curl up in the old chair beside the window and wrap myself in a blanket. The street is deserted outside. Later, I hear Duncan come in to the same sad creak of rusted hinges. I stay quiet so he doesn't realise I'm awake. Maybe he bothers one of the other girls. They built these old houses well and the walls are good and thick so you can't hear what is going on in the night once everyone is inside. Outside the window I watch the seagulls nesting on the roof of the tenement over the road and then the rain starts, hammering against the window like a rough kind of lullaby. I nod off quickly after that, without even getting into bed.

The next morning it's still raining. The haar on the firth has obliterated Fife. Duncan is in the photo booth when I get there, but we both know there'll be no business today. This is one of the perks of the job – frequent days off. There's nothing even Duncan can do about the erratic Scottish weather.

We walk along the Prom – the lights are off in Ferrari's, I note. Violetta would usually be in by now, switching on the coffee machine and firing up the gelato mixer in the back. Duncan and I make it to the arcade where Big Rob

McGuigan plonks mugs of tea on the counter with a bag of sugar and a single spoon. Barbra tells me that she's heard Yolanda Ferrari has been admitted to the Royal Infirmary on account of nervous stress. It doesn't take much to put one thing together with another, and I realise that the nervous stress is probably about Violetta and Henry. Yolanda has always been kind to me so, once I've had my tea, I decide go over to the hospital with a bunch of flowers. When I get there I can see that a lot of people have had this idea. Yolanda's sisters are knitting on chairs by the bed surrounded by a sea of bouquets and there is a young priest in a cassock next to Mr Ferrari – Victor – who is standing by the door.

Yolanda grasps my hand, 'Darling Rosie,' she says, 'have you heard?'

'Giorgio told me,' I reply as reverently as I can manage. 'I bumped into him last night outside the Plaza.'

'Oh . . . what to do?' Yolanda says, and starts wringing her hands together so dramatically that one of her sisters picks her way through the flowers and pours her a glass of water. 'How could she?' Yolanda moans. 'How could she? Can't you speak to her, dear?'

I lay the flowers on the end of the bed. 'It's a difficult thing to come to terms with all right,' I say.

Yolanda starts to howl. 'They're getting married in a registry office,' she cries. 'It's a mortal sin. A mortal sin, Father,' she directs herself to the priest, who comes over to the bed and says 'Now, now, Mrs Ferrari,' clearly not feeling that Violetta and Henry's choice of wedding venue, mortal sin or not, is worth becoming hysterical about.

I notice that Mr Ferrari has turned pale. This is a

serious proposition because during the whole of my childhood – all the time I have known Victor Ferrari, he has always looked as if he has just come back from holiday. A second later I can see why he's on the white side, because Violetta and Henry walk into the room cool as a pair of cucumbers. You could cut the silence with a knife. Yolanda stops howling and sits up in bed with her mouth open, and the sisters stop knitting and the priest freezes.

'Hi Ma,' says Violetta and she casually takes a seat right by the bed as if this whole palaver is nothing to do with her and she's just visiting a nice old lady in hospital out of the goodness of her heart. The diamond daisy is sparkling on her finger. I have to say, it looks good. 'Ma,' Violetta says with more confidence than I've ever seen her in possession of before, 'I know this decision is been tough on you. I know you and Papa have always tried to do the best for me. But you have to stop this right now. I love Henry. He loves me. And we are getting married. Can't we all just be happy about it?'

Victor Ferrari tenses up further. I can see he is about to fix things the only way he knows how, and I think that it is just as well for Henry that he is in a hospital and will receive prompt medical attention. Mr Ferrari is not the sort of bloke you want to mess with. Once, when there was a disagreement over the placement of rubbish bins on the back lane, he laid down Big Rob McGuigan and that is no mean feat. However, Yolanda has a different plan. She puts her hand up to stop her husband, and sinks into the pillows propping her up. 'My blood pressure,' she says, weakly.

Violetta gives her a sideways glance. 'Ma,' she says, 'give Henry a chance, won't you?'

'But you can do so much better,' Yolanda insists. 'The Fabrizis . . .'

Violetta sighs. 'I know. They make the best cones. Sliders too. Sugar cones and ice cream. A marriage made in heaven. In the last century, perhaps.'

'But that's how it's always worked,' her mother objects. 'When you work together, you're a real part of each other's lives. Giorgio's mother developed the recipe for their cones – her family were biscuit makers in Abruzzi and his father—'

'Yes, yes,' Violetta cuts in, 'his father's father sold penny licks in Milan. I know. But Mama, I make a vanilla that's better than anybody's.' Here, her eyes meet Henry's and I can see that Henry is good for her. Really good. Not as in a good provider or that he'll make a good father to her kids or that he's in a position to provide sugar cones of exceptional quality to her family business – but that he's good for her just as she is, which is to say that he believes in her. I might have known that when Violetta kept a secret it would be a doozy. 'I'd make the best sorbet too,' she says, almost as if she's flirting. 'If you'd let me. We don't need a marriage to make it work, Ma. Really.'

Victor Ferrari lets out a whelp. 'Sorbet,' he says dismissively and gestures, as if trying to pull the right words out of the air. 'It's just flavoured ice,' he adds. 'People won't pay for that. Where's the talent in sorbet?'

'It's cheap to make,' Violetta makes her case. 'And it's good for things like rhubarb – what else are you going to make with rhubarb, Papa, when it's in season and we can buy it in bulk for pennies?'

Mr Ferrari sighs. But Violetta is on a roll.

'I want to make marshmallows. And our own fruit jellies,' she exclaims. 'And nougat. We could be doing so much more. I want to open a booth on the High Street,' she continues. 'I'm going to make ten flavours and sweets. There are lots of tourists up there, you know. Not only with this new summer festival but even in the winter. Don't worry – I can still make gelato for your shop. And I'll work with Giorgio too if he's still willing.'

'Ten flavours,' says Yolanda weakly as if this is some kind of madness, worse perhaps even than the registry office. But she doesn't object any further and I realise that they're going to make peace. The Ferraris love Violetta – she's their only kid after all. And she and Henry make a handsome couple.

Outside the hospital, Giorgio is parked in a red Alfa Romeo Guilietta. It's flash but it suits him. I look at the car and think, 'That cost a lot of sliders,' and then he notices me. I wave and go over. It's drizzling still.

'They're going to get married in a registry office,' I tell him through the open window on the driver's side.

Giorgio snorts.

'Violetta is going to make ten flavours,' I add.

He gets a faraway look in his eye. 'It's the future. I think she's right about that,' he says and looks at the seat beside him where a bunch of carnations and roses lies wrapped in brown paper.

'Mrs Ferrari has a lot of flowers in her room,' I say. 'It looks like somebody died.'

'We're lucky nobody has yet,' Giorgio replies drily and I'm not sure if he's thinking about Mr Ferrari and what he'd like to do to Henry, or himself or maybe his own father.

'Tough guy,' I say because I figure it's generic.

Giorgio looks at me like I just agreed with him. 'Would you like to go for a coffee or something?' he says.

'Something,' I reply decisively and jump into the passenger seat, moving the flowers onto my lap. 'It's horrible out today.'

He turns on the engine and gets the windscreen wipers going. 'We could get lunch,' he suggests. 'I heard the Roxburgh Hotel is good. They have a carvery.'

I have no idea what a carvery is but it sounds fancy. The Roxburgh is in town, but if Violetta can raise her sights so can I. 'Great,' I say.

The Roxburgh is full of Italian waiters, of course. Some guy called Fabio embraces Giorgio like he's a long lost brother. Maybe he is. The place is quiet as he sees us to our seats. Three guys in the corner are chain smoking and drinking brandy as they knock out some kind of deal for a silver tea set, which they've bought at the auction rooms over the road. Two ladies perch on high stools at the bar, sipping saucers of champagne and nibbling from a dish of olives as they discuss a play they've seen. This festival thing is really taking off, I think. There are piles of leaflets by the door for all kinds of shows. Maybe I'll go to something.

'You're a rosebud,' Fabio says, flirtatiously, and kisses my hand before guiding me into a green velvet booth bounded by wooden fretwork with silk flowers stapled onto it. Giorgio doesn't bother with the menu. He just orders. I'm not sure what he says, because he speaks in Italian, but two plates of thinly sliced, rare roast beef, salad, chips and a bottle of red wine appear.

'Are you getting married, Rosie?' he asks as we try the wine.

I squirm a little. What comes into my mind is 'who'd want me?' That's how I feel about it. I mean Duncan wants me, of course. And sometimes I get carried away with one of the lads at the Plaza. It's safe these days and why shouldn't girls get their kicks too? They say they'll only give this new pill thing to married women but Barbra and I caught on fast. One of Barbra's pals works the pavement at the bottom of Constitution Street and the whores there take turns with a plain gold wedding ring and call themselves Mrs Dundee at a doctor's surgery out in Corstorphine where the GP is sympathetic. But what Giorgio is asking is quite a different thing. I can't see me doing housework and wrangling a couple of bairns. I'm not like Violetta.

Giorgio cops on fast too. 'You've got your photography,' he says. 'You're a career woman. I suppose the reason I asked is that you said Vi would be happy with . . .' Giorgio searches once more for the name of his rival.

'Henry,' I remind him. 'She'll be Mrs Campbell. And yes, I think she will happy.'

'But you don't think she'd have been happy with me?'

I pause. My mum says that guys are always a threat. My Dad certainly was. Victor Ferrari too. I have opportunities my Mum didn't – I got away from home and I have a job that keeps me. But some things don't change. Duncan is a source of both protection and danger. I'm not sure about Giorgio yet. I glance towards the door and wonder if he has set an elaborate trap in bringing me here.

'It seemed more like a business arrangement. A family thing between you,' I say, gently.

'Family,' he repeats and spears a chip.

Then a waiter starts setting the table next to us. It must be said he's what my Auntie Maureen would call 'fierce good looking.' Giorgio is distracted. It's almost as if he comes alive. I decide to take a chance. I lean across the table.

'There are different ways of looking at things, aren't there?' I say and I glance at the waiter and then back at Giorgio, so he knows that I know.

There's a moment suspended in time during which Giorgio looks as if he might explode. I eye my bag and make a quick calculation about how long it would take me to get through the door and down to Princes Street where there's a policeman directing the traffic and I can get a bus back to the sea. Giorgio lays down his cutlery. He turns away from the man laying the table and regards me as if he's sizing me up. Then he relaxes.

'Of course you'd see,' he says. He lets out a laugh that sounds almost good humoured. 'You're a camera, aren't you? You see everything.'

This isn't absolutely true. People think cameras

photograph the truth – things as they are – but cameras only photograph what you let them see. Which is quite a different thing. I've seen couples bickering, being really nasty to each other, and then I roll up and they smile like they're in love for the snap. I've seen skinny kids who turn up in shoes with no socks looking like millionaires when I print their image. It's a projection if you want it to be. Not the truth as it is.

'When did you realise?' he asks. 'About me?'

'When you shook my hand in Ferrari's,' I say. I might as well be honest.

And then Giorgio does something that takes me aback. He leans in and he kisses me – right on the lips. It's a stellar kiss too. I feel as if I'm falling through space. Through the stars. I lean into the booth. As Giorgio pulls away Fabio is polishing glasses behind the bar, watching us. He looks delighted. 'But,' I say, confused. 'I thought . . .'

Giorgio grins. 'I'd have given her kids, you know. The thing is that I like everything,' he admits. 'I like people. But the truth is I'm not prepared to give some of them up.'

'Settle down, you mean?'

'I'll never settle down. Not like that. I need . . . variety. For me, that's normal.'

'Violetta would hate that. She's conventional in every way – except about ice cream,' I say with a smile.

'I suppose I'd have hidden it from her,' he says.

I cast him a look that makes it clear that this is a terrible idea. Well it is, isn't it?

★

After lunch we walk down to Princes Street Gardens
past the Ross Bandstand where the audience is made up
of enthusiastic eight year olds, singing along with a man
who is dressed like a milkmaid with red grease paint on
his cheeks like some kind of technicolor misprint. Beside
the gallery there are jugglers and two women acting out a
scene from Shakespeare, right there in the street.

'I like you, you know,' Giorgio says. 'I like it here too.
Edinburgh is a nice city.'

I glance up at the Castle. I'm not so sure he'd like
it in the lee of the hill on the other side, or down the
Canongate where families live crowded into medieval
buildings that the Council really ought to knock down. I
figure I was lucky to be brought up near the sea. One of
the two women who are busking gets down on one knee
and starts reciting a poem. She kisses the other woman's
hand. Georgio is standing back, just looking at my face.

'You too,' he notes with one of his sunshine smiles.

For a moment I tell myself that I don't know what he's
talking about, but I do. Of course I do. Amy Harrison's
dresses used to take my breath away the last year of school.
I still have the pictures I took of her, dog-eared now, stuck
in the back of my journal.

Violetta and Henry's wedding happens so quickly that
there's gossip round Portobello that Violetta is knocked
up. Barbra overhears the milkman telling the postman
that it's a shotgun wedding, which is so far from the truth
it's laughable. It remains the case that Victor Ferrari would
do just about anything to stop his daughter marrying

Henry Campbell and it turns out the Campbells are equally opposed. Violetta and Henry set up a meeting between the two families, which, after a stilted, silent start, ends in an hysterical disaster with Yolanda bursting into tears because Violetta is marrying a Protestant, and Mrs Campbell crying silently into her handkerchief on the other side of the table because she doesn't want Henry marrying a Roman Catholic. Afterwards I meet Giorgio in the Cullen. He can't believe we all went to school together because this kind of thing, apparently, does not happen in Glasgow where Protestants and Catholics stay in what he refers to as 'their own lanes'.

'It's 1961,' I say. 'What are you on about?'

And meantime, Henry's as good as his word and buys a top-floor flat on Abercromby Place. Violetta and I climb onto the roof where there is a flat area. She brings up a Bush reel-to-reel tape recorder that she's plugged in downstairs on a long lead, and flicks the machine on to play this song called 'Nobody I Know' that her cousin in Liverpool recorded at his friend's gig in some place called the Cavern Club. I like it and we start dancing, not too near the edge. 'What's the band's name?' I ask. Violetta picks up the cover – 'It just says, The Beatles,' she shrugs. 'They're good, aren't they?' Afterwards she plays another by a girl called Priscilla White. Liverpool sounds like fun, I think. Maybe I ought to go there, with my camera, on a busman's holiday.

Far below, I can see the Castle in one direction but the standout view is down the hill and across to Fife in the other. I snap Violetta, the wind whipping her dark hair across her smiling face with the firth in the background, and Portobello only a hazy wisp further east, like some kind of dream. Nobody wants the top floors here, she tells me, because it used to be where the servants lived. But quite apart from the view and the light, the flat is like a palace inside. Henry bought a huge, American refrigerator with an ice-box that took over an hour to haul up the stairs. 'It was either that or a three-piece suite,' Violetta admits, 'so we'll have to sit on the floor for a while.' I figure they've got their priorities squared away, especially when Violetta brings out a tub of raspberry and mint sorbet, which we eat dangling our legs across the kitchen windowsill.

'Your dad is in for a shock,' I say.

Violetta nods. 'Sorbet is a more intense flavour,' she adds as if she's a theatre critic reviewing a play. 'He still doesn't get it. Ice cream is soothing but sorbet perks you up, don't you think?'

When the big day dawns, it's sunny. I work all morning at the photo booth and nip home after lunch to change. Violetta's not having bridesmaids so I'm as close as it gets and she's asked me to bring my camera and take some pictures for posterity. There's only going to be a dozen guests and, weirdly, Giorgio is one of them. He picks me up in the red Alfa Romeo Giulietta with the top down. I feel like Sophia Loren as I climb in and hold onto my big straw hat as we speed into town. Violetta looks like a princess, in a white, full, tulle skirt and a plain bodice.

She's wearing flowers in her hair – giant daisies. But you'd think it was Yolanda getting married, the way the attention is going. Henry's folk fade into the background like sepia prints while Yolanda, resplendent in a vibrant purple two-piece suit, bought for the occasion from Valente's on Queensferry Road, tries not to cry through the whole ceremony in such a way as to make sure everyone knows she'd really like to cry through the whole ceremony. She's still sniffing dramatically in the pub afterwards while Victor efficiently buys rounds of drinks at the bar. I know they'd have liked a huge wedding but things being what they are, it's best to keep it quiet.

We see the happy couple off at the door about six o'clock. The honeymoon is in a fancy hotel near Dunbar where the beach is wilder than Portobello and there isn't a Prom to speak of. I take a final picture of Violetta, bundling her skirts into the back of a taxi looking like a film star – the happiest I've ever seen her in my life.

In the bar, Henry's parents leave, or rather, evaporate, while Victor fetches Yolanda's coat. 'I know it isn't what you wanted,' Giorgio hugs her, 'but Vi will be fine. We all will,' he says. It's sweet of him to look after the Ferraris, I think. After the parents have gone home, he and I abandon the Alfa Romeo on Princes Street and take a walk. Giorgio produces a key for the private gardens along Queen Street and I take photographs of him, the evening sun like honey on his skin and a copse of sycamore trees in the background.

'What about your parents?' I ask. After all, they must be disappointed too.

Giorgio shrugs. 'You were right when you said it wouldn't be fair on Vi. You're some bird, Rosie.'

I put down my camera. The grass is lush here and it's private. Up the other end of the park an old lady is walking very slowly with a long-eared dog scampering around her feet. My chest feels suddenly tight and all I can see is a series of pictures that I haven't taken – Duncan bearing down on top of me, Big Rob with a black eye, my mother, crying, telling me to get out, get away. And then I start crying too. Not picturesque crying but red-eyed and snottery, gasping for breath, on my knees on the perfect lawn. At the other end of the park is Abercromby Place and the life Violetta will be coming back to. It feels miles and miles away – almost unreachable, like I could walk all my life and never get there.

Giorgio doesn't do what a gentleman ought to and hand me his handkerchief and say 'there, there'. He doesn't ask what's wrong. Instead, he just takes over. It's as if I've drowned in my own tears and he picks me up like I'm a kid out of her depth in the water, and carries me to a bench where he wraps his arms round me and mutters in Italian. I don't know what he's saying but it sounds nice.

'Sorry,' I get out when I can breathe again.

Giorgio pulls back. 'It's like you blossomed,' he says. 'Fabio's right. It's like you're a flower that came out.'

This is kind of him because I know for a fact that right now I don't look like any kind of flower – or if I do it's a daffodil that's been battered in a storm or a pale rose from a bouquet, smeared in muddy water and trampled after a wedding.

'I can get you out,' Giorgio offers. 'If you want to leave.'

My eyes fill with tears again. 'What?' I say.

I can't believe he knows. How could he know? He only breezed into town a couple of weeks ago. But it turns out Giorgio can see things as they are, just as much as I can. He's a camera too.

'You've got talent,' he continues and I wonder if he'd say that if I weighed 200lbs and looked like the bearded lady in the deckchair. Giorgio however, does not address my silent question. 'I've been thinking,' he continues, 'almost every ice cream parlour I know would sell your cards. We'd have to provide a rack, of course, and you'd need to shoot a few more pictures that feature ice cream, but that's a lot of cards, Rosie. It's a lot of money. Say you make tuppence off every one . . . I mean you'd be set.'

I nod. Then I stop. He's so handsome it's difficult to believe that he'd be tough enough for this. Duncan after all has put a few guys in hospital over the years. It'd be a shame for Giorgio to end up with his sunshine smile more of a sunset. Giorgio leans back. 'It won't be me,' he says reading my mind again. 'I know this guy called Dante O'Donnell. He's a fixer.'

'Dante O'Donnell?' I repeat.

'Italian-Irish,' Giorgio says. 'They say his fists are like the circles of hell.' He laughs. 'Dante's a good fighter but from what I understand, he prefers to talk you into whatever the proposition might be. I'm not asking you to marry me,' he adds.

'But you might make a ha'penny off every card . . .' I

feel like Frank Sinatra, heading on stage in Las Vegas.

'Do you think people would buy cards in fish and chip shops?' Giorgio wonders out loud.

I doubt it. People on the market for an ice cream are feeling whimsical about their holiday by the seaside, but people in fish and chip shops are mostly hungry.

'You could do a range for interiors. Framed prints,' Giorgio adds.

I have money saved up. Not enough. I wonder if I can rent one of those top floors that nobody wants and make the kitchen into a darkroom. 'Are you offering to . . . invest?' I ask him, square.

'Yeah. I'll help,' he says and he squeezes my hand. 'One for all, and all for one. Peace and love.'

Peace and love. I mean, as if that's important. I look more than a little sceptical.

'My American cousins are always going on about peace and love,' Giorgio adds. 'They say it's the coming thing.'

It's getting late. Theatregoers are heading home down Dundas Street and the sun is sinking in the west, like the sky is melting butter. I wonder if I'm going to end up sleeping on this park bench, because I'm not going back, I realise. I have my camera and that's all I need. Giorgio walks up to Hanover Street and puts in a call to Dante O'Donnell from a telephone box and apparently that's the whole thing set in train. I wonder momentarily if I've jumped from the frying pan into the fire, but I'm pretty sure it'll be better in the flames than it was in the hot fat – if it comes to that.

'Come on,' says Giorgio, 'I know a place. Let's get a drink and some dinner.'

The next morning it's raining again and he takes me to an estate agency to see about finding a flat in town. At the station on Princes Street I post a card to Barbra at the arcade. I choose one with a picture of the castle, but I can see what Giorgio means about a gap in the market – I'd rather send something more fun. 'Hope everything is OK on the Prom,' I scribble. 'See you soon.' I sign it with a flourish and pop it in the box. A kind of invitation. I suppose we'll see.

AUTHOR BIOGRAPHIES

ANNE HAMILTON

Anne Hamilton is an editor and a creative writing tutor. Originally a social worker and epidemiologist, she then gained a PhD in Literature and Creative Writing from the University of Glasgow. Anne's first book was the travel memoir, *A Blonde Bengali Wife*, inspired the Bangladesh-based charity, Bhola's Children, of which she remains a trustee. Anne won the Irish Novel Fair 2021, and is currently working on a novel. She lives in Edinburgh with her young son.

NADINE AISHA JASSAT

Nadine Aisha Jassat is a poet, writer and creative practitioner. She is the author of poetry collection *Let Me Tell You This* (404 Ink), has been widely published in anthologies and literary magazines, and was named in Jackie Kay's International Literature Showcase Selection of 10 Compelling BAME writers working in the UK. She received a prestigious New Writers Award from the Scottish Book Trust, and was shortlisted for the UK's largest poetry prize, the Edwin Morgan Poetry Award.

ALEXANDER McCALL SMITH

Alexander McCall Smith is one of the world's most prolific and most popular authors. His various series of books have been translated into over forty-six languages and have sold more than 30 million copies across the world. These include the *No. 1 Ladies' Detective Agency* series, the *44 Scotland Street* novels, the Isabel Dalhousie novels and the Von Igelfeld series. He also writes stand-alone novels, poetry, children's fiction and libretti for short operas.

IAN RANKIN

Born in Fife in 1960, Ian Rankin graduated from the University of Edinburgh in 1982, and then spent three years writing novels when he was supposed to be working towards a PhD in Scottish Literature. His first Rebus novel was published in 1987, and the Rebus books are now translated into twenty-two languages and are bestsellers on several continents.

SARA SHERIDAN

Sara Sheridan writes the popular 1950s Mirabelle Bevan Murder Mysteries as well as historical novels. An established equality campaigner, her book, *Where are the Women,* remaps Scotland according to women's history to memorialise our forgotten foremothers. In 2014 she was named one of the Saltire Society's 365 Most Influential Scottish Women past and present. Her 2021 publications include *The Fair Botanists*, set in 1820s Edinburgh and Mirabelle's ninth mystery, *Celtic Cross,* set in a Scottish nunnery in 1959.

IRVINE WELSH

Irvine Welsh was born in Edinburgh. He is the author of twelve novels including the international bestseller *Trainspotting* and its sequel *Porno*, both adapted into iconic films by Danny Boyle. His most recent novel *Dead Men's Trousers* continues the *Trainspotting* story. Welsh enjoys a dedicated global readership, tweets prolifically and serves as an Official Ambassador of the Homeless World Cup.

ABOUT ONECITY TRUST

The OneCity Trust was established as a result of a report commissioned by the Lord Provost of Edinburgh in 1998, to determine the extent of social exclusion and inequality within Scotland's Capital city. A key recommendation was the formation of an 'inclusion trust' and the OneCity Trust was duly established by a deed of trust dated 7 March 2003.

Nearly twenty years later, the Trust remains committed to supporting charitable and constituted groups within the city; working together by advancing, facilitating, and promoting the education, social welfare, human rights and the tackling of extreme inequalities in income and alleviation of poverty. Social exclusion and inequality are still evident within communities throughout the city, which has been exacerbated by the COVID-19 pandemic over the past two years.

The Trust continues to award financial grants but are also a conduit for funds, ideas and resources from local businesses, citizens and our Community Benefit partners, who together have helped us to continue to build the profile and grant making opportunities. In 2020/21, with our Community benefit partners, we were able to award grants to twenty-two organisations totalling £115,897.

OneCity Trust is thankful for the financial and pro bono support offered by a number of Community Benefit providers such as the City of Edinburgh Council, Travis

Perkins Managed Services, CGI UK Ltd, CCG (Scotland) Ltd, City Fibre, ENGIE Regeneration and Morrisons Energy Services.

Further information:
OneCity Trust
Lord Provosts Suite
City Chambers
High Street
Edinburgh
EH1 1YJ

Tel +44 (0) 131 469 3856
email admin@onecitytrust.com
Twitter @OneCitytrust
www.onecitytrust.com